Whom Shall I Kiss ...

An Earl, A Marquess, or A Duke?

Whom Shall I Kiss ...

An Earl, A Marquess, or A Duke?

Laura A. Barnes

Laura A. Barnes

2019

First Printing: 2019

ISBN: 9781796596793

Laura A. Barnes

www.l.uraabarnes.com

Cover Art by Cheeky Covers

Editor: Polgarus Studios

To all the sisters who are like best friends

And to all the best friends who are like sisters

Chapter One

"Are you positive you want to follow through with your plan, Sidney? What happens if your father discovers your experiment?"

"You worry too much, Phee. Papa is busy with his own research to even have a clue what I am about to do," Sidney Hartridge explained to her best friend Sophia Turlington.

Sidney understood Phee worried about what she set out to accomplish. Was it proper? Of course not. But then everything in society towards women was too proper. She wished to step outside the boundaries set for her and discover how far she could push the limits of etiquette. Why could gentlemen kiss who they wanted, when they wanted, and never a shameful word was whispered of them? However, if an unmarried lady did the same, society would ostracize her. If a gentleman didn't offer said lady a marriage proposal, then she disappeared to live in the country in disgrace. But if a gentleman made an offer for the lady's hand, then she would enjoy a life in the highest tiers of the aristocracy. Why couldn't a lady kiss who she desired and make the choice on who held her heart?

Not that Sidney looked to wed. She only wanted to conduct her own research on what choices were possible for her or any other debutante. She decided to open her dance card this season to every available gentleman in order to entice them to kiss her. She didn't tell Phee the full extent of her experiment. Phee thought Sidney wanted to know who might coax her into a kiss, but there was more to her analysis than a simple kiss. Sidney also wished to see which gentlemen would make an offer for her hand in marriage. She needed to expose the players of the ton when she finished her experiment. She'd watched too many of her friends destroyed by the scoundrels who graced the ballroom floors over the seasons. It fell to her to correct their wrongs.

Phee spotted the devious smile spreading across her friend's face as Sidney scanned the crowded ballroom, searching for her first prey. This idea was crazy. She knew Sid's heart was in the right place, but she was at real risk for ruination. However, Sidney, always jumped in feet first, and then thought with her head later. She was a passionate soul, something she inherited from both of her parents. Sidney's whole family fought for the underdog and offered their support where needed. Phee envied Sid's life and wished to be as adventurous as her. For now, she was content to watch from the sidelines. As Sidney's best friend, she had to be on guard and ready to help at a moment's notice.

Most people were not drawn to her beauty, but to her confidence instead. Phee wished for an ounce of Sid's self-assurance. As she continued to regard her friend, she noted Sidney's attire for the evening. Phee laughed to herself as she took in Sid's dress.

The new creation of pink chiffon and silk made her appear sweet and demure. The top of her gown was simple, with a scoop neckline that covered her breasts respectfully, yet still snug. To the matrons it appeared prim, but up close, men could appreciate the tightness of the garment. It would then lead their imaginations in unrespectable directions. A forest green bow wrapped around her waist, and her full skirts bounced when she moved. Dainty slippers adorned her feet, peeking out as Sid tapped her foot in anticipation. While the dress screamed pure, her features yelled siren. Her maid had interwoven a string of pearls between the luxurious, auburn curls piled atop her head.

However, it wouldn't be her appearance that enticed the gentlemen to her side this evening, but the lure of her eyes. Usually, Sid wore her spectacles to scare away any potential suitors. Tonight, she discarded them, and her sensuous, dreamy stare would reel them into her plans.

Sidney surveyed the crowd, noting the gentlemen in attendance. This evening held the opening event of the season. Anybody with the highest ranks in the ton graced the ball with their presence. Sidney had marked her potential victims before she arrived. Two of them were present, and the last one should present himself before the evening concluded.

As Sidney ran her palms along her gown, straightening her bow, she knew her dance card would be full as soon as she stepped out from behind these columns. Her usual attire of a plain dress with a high collar and her customary glasses always planted her in the wallflower section. But this ball would be different. The eligible men would beg for a chance to dance with her. Tonight would set the first stage of her experiment into motion. She turned to her friend and grabbed her hand, pulling them into the festivities.

"Stage one, Phee." Sidney laughed with excitement.

Phee groaned at her friend's enthusiasm. This season would not be dull by any standard. She must keep Sidney out of too much trouble though. In doing so, she hoped she was not the one who became engulfed in a scandal.

Sidney strode amongst the ton, wearing an expression of innocence, placing herself amongst the elitist of the aristocracy. She could do this because the Prince Regent, Prinny himself, highly regarded her family. Her father's interaction with the Crown positioned their family well. They were sought after to appear at all the ton's functions. Sidney never attended unless her mother forced her. She knew her mama wanted to see her married off rather than engulf herself in her father's research. So, to pacify her mother, she attended a few balls and musicals and befriended the wallflowers. But as she observed her friends fall to ruin year after year, she knew she had to halt the double standards of their society.

The hostess greeted Sidney and introduced her to a line of gentlemen, who filled her dance card full. Only one of her subjects approached her, claiming a waltz of all dances. Sidney smiled at him as he penned his name, his gaze taking in the tightness of her gown around her breasts instead of meeting her eyes. Men were so predictable. This experiment would be easier than she expected. She suspected that this particular gentleman would sign her dance card; he could never resist a beauty to seduce. He would be the most fun to play with throughout her study. The gentleman was soon nudged aside for another eager fool requesting a dance.

They all gathered amongst her, the simpering fools they were. These same gentlemen ignored her any other night because of her dowdy dress and plain features. When she dropped her familiar appearance and graced her form with the added enhancements, they clamored around her like pups begging for a treat. She giggled at their attempts at flattery until the orchestra started with the first set of the evening. The first man who signed her card strutted through her group of admirers, claimed her hand, and swept her toward the dance floor.

Sidney inwardly rolled her eyes at her dance partner's performance of dominance, but smiled and nodded her head in agreement as he boasted about himself. She took mental notes to write in her journal later as she studied how the male species interacted with other dancers on the floor. She was going mad listening to this pompous jackass brag about himself. Were all the gentlemen of rank always this conceited with themselves? This could be another variable she needed to add to her study; it could help explain her hypothesis that men thought women were impressed by their status in the ton.

As the dance finished, her partner reluctantly passed her to the next gentleman on her list, only for her to be bored again by another male infatuated with himself. If this was how the season proceeded, Sidney would require a distraction to endure this torture. She didn't have the same patience as her friend Sophia, who would have drawn these gentlemen out of their arrogance to dote on her. Phee held the special gift of charming people to see past themselves and to think of others.

Once the dance ended, her partner escorted her near the windows, trying to coax her outdoors for a breath of fresh air. Since he was not one of her subjects, she begged off, pleading the need for a drink. The gentleman wanted to please her, so he ran off to do her bidding. Sidney rolled her eyes again at his eagerness. She needed to stop this habit, or her eyes would ache from all the rolling they would endure if every dance ended in this fashion.

Sidney reached into her reticule, pulling out her fan to cool herself. With each swish of the fan against her warm body, she noted the mating ritual taking place on the ballroom floor. The gentlemen and ladies flirted with each other shamelessly. It did not matter if they weren't married to one another, as long as their egos were stroked. Sidney noticed another subject flirted from one woman to the next, drawing out the seduction in open display. He would be her most successful subject, already proving her experiment a success with his prowess. She waited impatiently for their dance later this evening.

Sid stood on her tiptoes, searching the area for Phee, finding her standing beside her mother. Sidney swiftly lowered herself, hoping Phee didn't catch sight of her. It wasn't that she didn't want to enjoy the ball with her best friend, she just didn't want to stand next to Lady Turlington. Phee's mother was a dragon—a fire breathing one at that. Lady Turlington felt Sidney was poorly neglected by her parents and always tried to better her. While it held true, Sidney's parents were a bit absentminded and were usually too busy in their own pursuits to pay her any attention. It didn't mean they were awful parents. It was quite just the opposite. They were the most loving parents a girl could ask for. Not only loving but also supportive.

"What trouble are you involved in now, Brat?" a voice whispered in her ear.

Sidney stilled at the tone; another one of her subjects had arrived. Her plan kept falling into place. She turned around slowly to catch his reaction to her appearance. When she faced him, she wasn't disappointed. The expression of brotherly companion changed to the stare of an appreciative male. The easy-going smile of friendship vanished, replaced with admiration of what was presented before his eyes. She placed the sweetest of demure smiles on her face and flashed him a glance of innocence.

"Why nothing, Rory, I am waiting for my dance partner to bring me a glass of lemonade," Sidney answered.

Sidney waited for a reply, only to watch as his eyes raked her form. He started at her toes and worked his way along her body, until he reached her chest, and then his eyes widened. His journey continued to her face, pausing at her smile, where his own face turned into a perplexed frown. When he finally reached her gaze, she saw his eyes glaring at her.

Earl Roderick Beckwith, known as Rory to his closest friends, remained in conflicted emotion as he stared at the woman before him. He, himself didn't know quite how to react to the sight. Before him stood a stunning creature in pink, smiling innocently—a vision held false, for he understood what lay beneath. Sidney was up to something; she didn't fool him with her smile. He knew better. Still, the allure surrounding her confused him. This was not the young chit he frequently debated issues with on a weekly basis. Standing before him was a lady who begged for a stroll around the ballroom floor, or a walk in the garden. Actually, for .... He must halt his mind from where his dangerous thoughts took him.

Sidney decided to add another element to her experiment. She wondered what the male's reaction would be if she offered them the same perusal, they in turn bestowed upon her? Her gaze traveled the same direction as his. She started at his shoes, where she noted the worn footwear hidden with shoe polish to appear more dignified. She knew Rory's family had fallen on rough times but he worked to replenish the family coffers. Her eyes took their time climbing past his long limbs and over his stomach and chest. He filled out a suit quite nicely. When she reached his face, she tilted her head to admire it for a while. While it turned most ladies away, others, like Sidney, admired his imperfections. Thick red-gold hair graced his head which curled around his ears. His nose was slightly out of joint from too many fights. His Irish heritage laid claim to that. His quick temper made him react with his fists instead of with his intellectual mind. When she glanced at his mouth, she noticed his smirk. Her eyes rose to his, where she took in his hazel depths twinkling at her in humor. She shrugged her shoulders at his reaction and gave him her own smirky smile.

"Well?"

"Well what?"

"What are you up to now?"

"I told you, I am waiting for a refreshment."

"Sidney, I understand you better than most of the guests here. Now I will ask you again, what are you—" he began only to be interrupted.

"I believe this is our dance."

"Why I believe you are correct, My Lord," Sidney replied.

Sidney turned toward Rory and nodded her head as her partner swept her away onto the dance floor.

Rory watched the couple line up for the next set. He continued to view them as she flirted with the young lord, noting how the fool practically drooled at her feet. He must keep an eye on her for the sake of her parents. They were like family to him, and if she entangled herself in trouble, he'd feel responsible. He needed to find Sophia to discover what mischief Sidney entangled herself in this time.

~~~~~~

The Duke of Sheffield stood nursing his drink as he watched his next partner have her toes stomped upon by her current dance partner. He wondered who the divine creature in pink chiffon and silk could be. He didn't recall ever dancing with her before. She held herself with a confidence most of the debutantes present tonight lacked. The lady would make an excellent duchess. As the last of the Sheffields, he had reached an age where it became expected of him to produce an heir and a spare. His grandmother's constant badgering about a wife and children reached the end of his nerves. To pacify her, he informed her he would secure a bride by the end of the season. So, this evening he decided to narrow his selection of possible candidates. No simple miss would do. She must have the credentials of a proper pedigree, be strong, and be supportive. Most of all, she must be beddable. He refused to marry himself off to a simpering cow to appease his grandmother. A chill ran along his spine at who his grandmother might saddle him with for a wife.

Alexander Langley continued his regard of the lady as she became agitated at her partner. He laughed out loud at her impatience as they swept past him. Perhaps, she wouldn't be a good candidate. When she glared at his humor, he lifted his glass to her with a twisted smile. Yes, she would be a pistol to fool around with, but not quite duchess material. At least he would enjoy holding her in his arms on the next dance. He would allow himself to have a pleasurable season; just because he decided to marry didn't make him a groom yet.

"Sheffield, who is that amazing creature you are admiring?" Marquess Noah Wildeburg, Wilde to his closest friends bumped into him. Wilde was already two sheets to the wind, and the ball had just begun. Alex shook his head at his friend's early demise. He must keep Wilde's attention away from the young chit or he wouldn't get his chance to dance with her. Sheffield already decided he wouldn't court her, but it didn't mean he couldn't flirt with her. If she met Wilde before him, he would never get the chance. Wilde always stole the beauties from him with his legendary charm. There wasn't a lady young or old who could resist him. He charmed every woman, from the crones of the ton to the wallflowers glued to the wall.

"Some new miss I'm amusing myself with as I watch the young pups fall all over her. Fools, all for a charming smile." Sheffield tried to discourage Wilde.

"Mmm, she appears to have more than a charming smile," Wilde stared after her, regarding her charms. "I wonder if her dance card is full?"

"Sorry, old chap, from what I hear it is full."

"Another time then. Care to join me in the card room?"

"I will be along shortly. I must escort Grandmother around the room."

Wildeburg winced at the thought of having the responsibility of another person to care for. He took one last look at the chit on the dance floor who caught his attention. She captivated more than his eye. As he looked around the crowded ballroom, he noticed she drew every male's attention to her as her dance partner tried to twirl her around the dance floor. The only thing the fool managed, was to bump her into the other couples as they danced. He saw her patience wore thin by the brittle smile upon her lovely face. A face he could stare at for hours if he was that sort of chap. When the fool bumped her against a column and preceded to step on her toes, Wilde decided to take pity on the beauty. Since he was near them, of course, they were practically at his feet.

"Let me be of some assistance. You seem to be in a spot of trouble," he said as he swooped in and transferred her into his arms.

The bloke stuttered a response, which only became drowned out by the orchestra as Wilde swept the young miss away across the dance floor. He glanced down to smile his accomplishment at the miss, only to see her scowl deepen.

"Who do you think you are, sir, to interrupt my dance?"

"Now is that any way to thank me for rescuing you from broken toes?"

"My toes are not broken, nor were they at any risk to become broken."

"I disagree with you, my dear. From where I stood, you were at a risk of an injury to your person. A very delightful person at that," he drawled as his eyes took notice of her loveliness.

Sidney's anger simmered below the surface as she listened to the arrogance of her new dance partner. Not only did he interrupt her experiment, he also had the audacity to expect her to thank him. In addition to his faults, she could also add he devoured her with his eyes. His gaze traveled the length of her body up and down, then back again. With every glance, they lingered near her breasts, and when not there, he stared into her eyes. He behaved as a scoundrel of the highest order. A rogue who wished one thing from her, in which she would never grant. Sidney recognized he would be a perfect specimen for her experiment, but her frustration toward him affected her train of thought.

It wasn't only her frustration that distracted her; it was the touch of his hands against her waist. While he acted like a gentleman, when he held her hand and gently placed his other hand at her hip, his touch heated her insides. The warmth spread from his fingertips as it seeped into her. She felt flustered. His touch was nothing compared to the smile lighting his eyes. They were devilish and full of humor that wrapped her in his charm. His eyes begged her to laugh with him of the situation she had found herself in. These emotions were new to her, something she should explore but hesitant to respond to. She needed to be cautious, for she was held in the arms of a gentleman who could break her heart if she allowed him to charm her. Sidney tamped down her reaction to him and let her analytical brain take over. She could play on these emotions in retrospect for her experiment, use the allure she felt and apply it to her theory.

Wilde became cautious as the chit's expression changed from one of anger to one of flirtation. She coyly lifted her lips into a sensuous pout while her eyes darkened to a midnight blue. Did he glimpse desire in those depths? He was caught unaware at her transformation, unprepared for the siren she became, and he stumbled when he stepped on her toes like the dance partner he had rescued her from. No wonder the bloke behaved as a bumbling idiot toward her if she had smiled at him like she smiled at him now. But her smile was nothing compared to the husky laugh floating between her kissable lips. Lips he wanted to taste. Her laugh touched him deeply, making him want to hear more. He never felt this instant attraction for any other lady. She wasn't his usual flavor. He preferred the widows of the ton, not the silly debutantes. Wilde trifled with them from time to time if the attraction presented itself—who was he to refuse temptation? He avoided the parson's noose like the plague and only fooled around with those he knew wouldn't trap him. As delightful as this chit seemed to be, he needed to leave. It was either that, or he would embarrass them both by kissing her endlessly on the ballroom dance floor.

"You are correct, sir. Please accept my apology for doubting your true intentions. You are a hero of the highest order," Sidney cooed.

The orchestra finished playing the current set and prepared for a waltz. He dropped his hands from around her, putting distance between them. She held her hands in front of her primly as she tilted her head, studying him. Her rescuer was tall with thick, honey blond hair and bedroom eyes which held promises of pleasure. He stepped back from her, and she took a small step toward him. Her gaze shifted behind him, and her eyes lit up even more, if it were possible. She then took two more steps toward him, and he panicked. He retreated only to smack into somebody standing at his back. A hand halted him from falling backward.

"I believe this waltz is mine." Wilde heard the familiar voice of his friend talking to the beauty.

Sidney lifted her dance card and noted the Duke of Sheffield to be her next dance partner. Alexander Langley stood behind the man, who she decided would make an excellent addition to her research. Especially as she had just witnessed his reaction to her change of attitude. He wanted to flee from her as fast as he could. She decided to have a little fun with the two gentlemen who stood before her, purely for the sake of research. She needed to understand how jealousy played a part in how a gentleman pursued a lady.

"You are correct, Your Grace, but would you mind giving me a moment to thank this kind gentleman for his assistance?"

Sheffield stood offended that this miss would make him wait for a dance he offered. Did she not realize who he was? He knew he should have moved on from her—she wasn't duchess material—but the smile she bestowed on him drew him to her bidding. She smiled sweetly at him while she twisted her fingers before her, obviously nervous that she offended him. At the sight of her discomfort, he changed his mind to the dance. He would wait. If he acknowledged the truth of the matter, he became more annoyed at how she wanted to thank his friend. He thought Wilde had wandered to the card room, but instead he followed the beauty. He should have known better where his friend was concerned. There wasn't a skirt safe from his pursuits. He squeezed harder on Wilde's shoulder, expressing his irritation with him.

"By all means. I will await your presence for our dance."

Wilde cringed at the edge in Sheffield's voice to the miss. He knew the frustration that simmered under the surface. Her actions irritated Sheffield because, as a duke, she had shoved him to the side for a mere marquess—one who wasn't very honorable. He only rescued the chit for a chance to fool with her, and Alex recognized his intentions. But it all changed as he held her in his arms. He wanted more but realized he shouldn't. He needed to leave.

"Thank you, My Lord, for your kindness. If you so desire, I have one dance remaining on my card you can request."

Wilde bowed before her. "It was a pleasure, my dear, to rescue a damsel in distress. I am sorry I cannot accept your lovely offer; a prior engagement requires my attention. I wish you a lovely evening, My Lady."

He raised her hand to his mouth for a kiss upon her gloved fingers. Wilde felt the small tremble as his lips lingered. When he lifted his eyes to her gaze, he drowned in their dark depths. With a growl heard from his side, he dropped her hand and bowed to her. Before she could respond he turned and strode out of the ballroom.

Sidney's hand slowly dropped to her side as she watched him disappear. Her thoughts became jumbled as she recalled his stare. She pressed her hand to her side, soaking in his touch. The notes of the orchestra as they played the waltz shook her out of her state of confusion.

Chapter Two

"If you are ready, My Lady." The duke held out his hand to her.

Sidney laid her palm in his in her dreamlike state as he whisked her toward the dance floor. The dance, a mixture of twists and turns, made her concentrate on it instead of the man who had swiftly left her company. There were too many distractions tonight keeping her from what she hoped to accomplish. After this dance with the duke, she needed to find Phee and gather her thoughts.

"You have me at a disadvantage, for you know my identity, but I am clueless to yours." Sheffield smiled at the distracted beauty, hoping to draw her attention back to him.

"But sir, we have met on several occasions before. Why, only last week we discussed women being allowed to continue their education at university, where you disagreed with my viewpoint. Papa ordered me to leave the room so as not to upset you," Sidney replied.

Sheffield halted for a moment in their dance then swept her around in a circle. His eyes not believing the words she spoke. This couldn't be the same chit whom he had argued with on a weekly basis. No, that miss was mousy and always wore glasses. This lady had long luxurious hair bound in enticing curls, and her eyes did not hide behind any lenses. Her gaze drew him in to the truth of her character. Still, he wasn't convinced as his eyes slowly traveled along her form. Pink chiffon and silk with a forest green bow adorned her body, hugging her small frame, different from the proper, plain day dresses he usually saw her in. As his eyes settled on her feet, he noticed the dainty slippers she danced in, not the usual clunky boots she wore as she stomped through her parents' garden. His eyes moved in reverse along her body and lingered on her breasts. He noticed how her tight bodice framed her body. He gulped and raised his eyes to hers, but he didn't meet her gaze because her eyes were busy granting him the same examination he was giving her. Her glance trailed the length of his body. Why the impudent chit, who did she think she was? Sidney Hartridge, of course, a lady who didn't follow the usual rules of the society. When she finished scrutinizing him and met his eyes, he raised a haughty ducal eyebrow at her display of vulgarity.

Sidney laughed at Sheffield's reaction to her perusal of his body. She had gathered so much data this evening. The duke had been clueless to her identity. She watched the shock of admiration turn to confusion as he looked her over.

"Lady Sidney Hartridge, Your Grace," she informed him in her sweetest voice.

"Yes, so you are. I apologize for not recognizing you."

"No need to apologize. I am aware of the difference in my appearance."

"May I enquire as to why the sudden change?"

"You may. It is Mama. She wishes to see me settle, and Papa agrees with her. I do not wish to be a burden on them any longer, so I agreed to let my mother dress me as a proper lady."

"Well the transformation is astounding. You are a lovely young lady."

"Thank you, Your Grace. Your compliments mean the world to me." Sidney took her research to the next level with the duke when she brought her hand off his shoulder. She slid her fingers under the lapel of his jacket to lightly caress him, then smoothed his suit before flashing him a flirtatious smile.

This time when Sheffield missed the steps of the dance it wasn't from mistaking her identity. Instead, her smile and the stroke of her fingers against his chest distracted him. He ended up making a fool out of himself like all the other gentlemen before him. Sheffield trounced on her toes and bumped them into another couple. He stared as her smile turned into a grimace of pain. Now he had become the bumbling pup. He drew her in closer as he corrected their steps and swept her over near the windows. With the doors open, he was able to dance them onto the terrace without drawing anybody's attention. Sheffield found an empty bench and lowered her to rest.

"It seems I owe you another apology. Not only did I not recognize you this evening, but I have stomped on your lovely toes."

Sidney lowered her lashes, a blush gracing her cheeks. The unexpected detour to the terrace flustered her. While this was a goal to reach in her research, it happened earlier than she expected. She hadn't prepared herself for being alone with any of her subjects. Let alone one, who for some reason also consumed her attention. While the attraction she felt toward Sheffield differed from what she felt for the gentleman before him, it was still an attraction. What she didn't understand was why she had never experienced this pull before. It wasn't as if this was their first meeting. They'd had countless discussions throughout the last few years. No, more like arguments. They were always on opposite sides of the debate.

When she didn't answer him, he sat on the bench next to her. He reached for her hand and held it between his. Her breath quickened and her heart beat faster.

"Are you well? Can I offer you refreshment?"

"No, I am fine. Thank you for your attendance and the lovely waltz."

Sheffield held her hands and felt her pulse rise at her wrist. As he watched her cheeks turn pink, he realized what a delightful gem she was. She contained many facets, and he was curious to learn more. Perhaps, Sidney Hartridge held the charms to be a duchess after all. Her family held one of the highest ranks in the ton, with her father being an adviser to the Crown. He knew from his past arguments with her that she was a strong-willed woman who would stand against his grandmother. He would have to adjust her behavior. Once they married, she would have to respect his authority. But, she had all the charms of an attractive young lady he felt a draw toward. Sheffield wanted to test the waters. He traced his gloved fingers across her wrist and felt her pulse beat more rapidly at his caress. He smiled at her sharp intake of breath. Yes, Sidney Hartridge would make an exceptional duchess, indeed.

Sidney gasped at his bold move. She stared as the domineering gleam lit his eyes as he stroked her wrist. While his touch sent warmth throughout her body, his male arrogance frustrated her. Her research finally came to the forefront of her mind. Was this how the scoundrels of the ton seduced the innocent wallflowers? If so, she understood how they were unable to resist their charms. Sidney herself had become a victim tonight, not once but twice. But it must end now, for she gathered enough information to get started. She needed to end this without scaring him away, though. She wanted to draw him into a chase. Sidney slid her hands away from him and pretended to act flustered as she fixed her bow.

The last notes of the waltz drifted from the balcony windows as the terrace started to fill with couples cooling off from the dance. Sheffield slid to the opposite end of the bench, so as not to draw attention their way. He nodded his head at couples as they walked past them. He needed to return her to her parents before any gossip started about them. While he was sure of his pursuit for her, he didn't need rumors to spread before he made a final decision. He rose from the bench and offered her his arm.

"Shall I return you to your mother?"

"Yes, please."

Sidney settled her hand in the crook of his arm as he escorted her inside. When Sheffield returned her to her parents, they were not alone. They stood with Sophia and her parents, along with Earl Roderick Beckwith. She noticed Rory's eyes narrow, seeing her on the arm of the Duke of Sheffield. They narrowed even more when he took in the blush across her cheeks. She must distract Rory before he ruined everything for her. She hoped the duke wouldn't linger to discuss her father's research.

Her eyes turned toward Phee, who motioned her head toward Rory and mouthed, "He suspects." Sidney gave a small nod in understanding and sent Phee a message of help with her eyes. The one good thing about being close friends was that Phee understood what she wanted without her having to say any words. Phee turned toward Rory and hinted that she wished to dance. Rory, being the ultimate gentleman, offered Phee his arm and escorted her onto the dance floor, but not before he sent a glare Sidney's direction.

"Sheffield, my good man, I see you coaxed our Sidney onto the dance floor this evening," her father shouted.

Her poor father was hard of hearing and spoke as if everybody else was too. While most fathers this action would have come across as a brag to others, but with him talking loudly was his normal behavior. Sidney winced as she saw the other members of the ton glared and humphed as they wandered away. But Sheffield knew of her father's lack of hearing and squeezed her hand in understanding as he replied in his usual friendly way.

"Yes, and a superb dancer she is. I must admit, I was overcome by surprise at her transformation."

"Yes, her mother is always trying to get her into those fancy dresses, and Sidney finally changed her mind this evening. We don't understand why, but it made her mother smile, and that is what matters."

"Well it has been my honor." Sheffield turned toward her and dipped his head. "A very sweet one," he whispered in her ear.

Sidney's blush grew even darker, if it were possible. Then as soon as he murmured in her ear, he wished her parents a pleasant evening and left their small group. She stared at him as he walked toward the card room. Did she really hold an attraction to the duke? Impossible. It must be the charm he wrapped around her.

"How kind of Sheffield to dance with you tonight, Sidney, considering how you tear him to pieces most of the time," her father commented.

"He was unaware of who I was, Father."

"What do you mean, dear?" asked Lady Hartridge.

"He didn't recognize me with my hair done and a lovely dress on," Sidney explained.

"Well, either way, you danced with the Duke of Sheffield tonight," her mother gushed.

Sidney smiled at her parents as they continued their discussion on how the duke behaved as a perfect gentleman. While Sidney agreed, she also witnessed the arrogant charm he displayed. She couldn't wait to return home to document her data. She obtained a lot of information this evening to get started with her research.

Phee and Rory returned to them after the danced ended. As Rory pulled Phee behind him, Phee shook her head for Sidney to beware. Rory stood at her side with a scowl upon his face while she smiled innocently back at him. Each of them stood their ground, waiting for the other to speak. When Sidney refused to talk, he grabbed her arm and turned to her parents.

"Sidney has promised me the next dance, please excuse us. I will return her to you at the end of our set," Rory informed them.

"Of course, how sweet of you to dance with Sidney too. She has been most popular tonight," her mother responded.

"Yes, she has, hasn't she," he muttered as he led them onto the dance floor.

They twirled for several notes before he drew her close to him in the middle of the dance floor. As other couples danced around them, they were hidden from the prying eyes of her parents. He swayed her to make it appear as if they danced, but Sidney sensed his frustration by the tenseness of his body.

"Whatever game you play, it needs to end now. You toy with two powerful men, one who could destroy your family, the other who could ruin you."

"Who was the other gentleman?"

"What? Did you not hear a word I have spoken?"

"Yes, yes. Destruction and ruination are in my future. Now spill, who is he?"

"Marquess Noah Wildeburg."

"The elusive Wildeburg danced with me? He never dances with anybody."

"Well it seems you charmed him from afar this evening."

This kept getting better and better. Absolutely perfect. She never imagined she could lure a rake like Wildeburg into her experiment. The data she collected from him would support her hypothesis. Now all she needed to do was to hold his interest, which shouldn't be too hard. She could tell he held an attraction to her, and she would use her allure to draw him in. Wait until Phee heard she danced with Noah Wildeburg. Wildeburg never danced, let alone talked, to the debutantes of the ton. Sure, there was the gossip of his pursuits as he chased a few. However, their families covered the relationships with engagements to other gentlemen or sent them far away to live with relatives. He preferred married women or widows. Rumors whispered in private spoke of him keeping two to three mistresses at a time, as his lust was ravenous. Sidney felt warm as she remembered his arms around her.

Rory watched the blush spread across Sidney's face and realized she had fallen for the scoundrel. He needed to put a stop to whatever her plans were. Wildeburg would ruin her in a heartbeat and walk away without a second glance. He owed it to the Hartridge's to keep Sidney out of trouble.

"Promise me you will stay clear of him, Sid."

"I can make no promises, Rory. If a gentleman requests a dance from me, it would be rude of me not to accept. You know I cannot risk offending anybody. The damage would fall on Papa."

Rory scowled, but she was correct. While her father held counsel for the Crown, they could wipe away his rank if anybody in his family offended the wrong peer of the aristocracy. And Wildeburg would be just the bloke to seek revenge. He was as wild as his name suggested. No gentleman or lady were safe from his charms, but if he withdrew his charms, then you had better hide. Sidney played with fire, and she was too innocent to know better.

"Then at least promise me you will be careful around Wildeburg and Sheffield."

"I promise, Rory. When did you become so protective?"

"When you started styling your hair and dressing like a princess."

Rory's compliment caused Sidney to blush again. It was the nicest thing he had ever said to her. He usually called her a brat and treated her like a kid sister. Now here he danced with her at a ball and called her a princess. Tonight was full of surprises. She didn't know how to respond to his kindness, so she dipped her head and stared at their feet as they finished their dance. Rory returned her to her parents, where he gave her a final look. Sidney didn't quite understand his stare. If she was more experienced, she would have thought it held a look of desire. When she tilted her head at him in question, he smiled wistfully before he left.

Phee came to stand at her side, waiting for Sidney to respond about her dance with Rory. Sidney remained at a loss at what to share with her. Oh, she had much to share, but she had no clue where to start. Plus, the crowded ballroom wasn't the place to discuss her research.

"Meet me at the park tomorrow. I have much I need to tell you."

"Are you all right, Sid? You seem lost."

Sidney turned to her friend, grabbing her hand, "Yes, dear. I am only processing all the data I have collected this evening."

"Have you changed your mind?"

Sidney laughed. "No, my mind is more determined than ever."

Phee watched the gleam in Sidney's eyes. When Sidney behaved in this manner, there would be no way of ever talking her out of the trouble she would surely get herself into. Maybe after Sid slept on this, she would change her mind. Oh, who was she fooling? The events from this evening had only set Sidney's mind in stone. She would have to make sure Sid avoided a scandal. Phee promised she would meet Sidney in the park in the morning and spoke her farewell.

As her friend walked out of the ballroom with her parents, Sidney turned to hers and asked if they could retire for the evening. She pleaded sore feet and exhaustion from dancing as her reason. It thrilled them that she'd had a successful evening, so they agreed. Her mother suggested she should get her rest because she was positive their receiving room would be full of potential suitors tomorrow. She inwardly groaned and hoped her mother's prediction would be false. Courting was the last thing she had time for, but she knew that she must take part in the age-old ritual for her project to be a success. If Sidney admitted the truth, part of her held a little curiosity on how many gentlemen would call on her tomorrow afternoon.

Chapter Three

Wilde lounged in the comfort of Sheffield's carriage. His friend knew how
to surround himself with the luxuries of life. There was nothing the duke
deprived himself. His every desire was catered to. Sheffield had to hold
himself at the highest esteem and appear to the ton that the very best in life
was within his grasp. If not, his peers would tear him apart. Wilde was
grateful he didn't have to hold himself to such a high example. Of course, he
must keep up appearances, but nothing as grand as Sheffield. He rubbed his
hand across the leather side, back and forth and he contemplated if he
should inquire after the young miss. If he asked, he risked offending him if
Sheffield considered her his future bride. Wilde knew his curiosity confused
him, but the need to know overrode his common sense.

"Will you at least inform me of her name?"

"What, in the time you spent in her company you didn't inquire for
yourself?"

"No, an attraction wrapped us in an embrace, and we were unable to
swap names with one another." Wilde decided the hell with angering him.
The game was on. He recognized possessive behavior when he saw it, and
Sheffield held an interest in the chit. He watched him come to attention at
the word "attraction."

"Keep away from her, Noah. She isn't your usual conquest."

"That is what makes her so interesting. She holds a certain charm I find desirable."

"Well you won't get the chance to taste her charm."

"So sure of yourself, are you?"

Sheffield looked at his fingernails, pretending boredom at Wilde's conversation, but he was anything but bored. He was at a crossroads. If he showed too much interest in the young lady, then Wilde would pounce on her. However, if he showed no interest at all, then Wilde would still pursue her. If he played against Wilde, he fought a losing battle. He would have to advance his game with Sidney Hartridge by impressing her before Wilde sank his charm into her and ruined her for any other man.

"Yes, as a matter of fact, I am. However, I am a fair man in the game of love. I will give you her name on one condition."

"Who said anything about love? I only wanted the chit's name for curiosity's sake, not to marry her. Good god, man, just forget it."

Sheffield smiled to himself at his strategic wording. He knew if he mentioned the word love, Wilde would run in the opposite direction. Nothing scared him more than love and marriage, which kept the young ladies of the ton safe. Wilde was a scoundrel of the worst order, and he would make a horrible husband with his gambling, drinking, and whoring. Yes, he would do Lady Sidney a favor and discourage Wilde from any interest in her. She would thank him later for this.

"Where do you want me to drop you off tonight? The usual spot?" Sheffield inquired.

"Yes, why not. A man needs to enjoy himself with some kind of pleasure before he calls it a night," Wilde replied.

Sheffield tapped his walking stick to the roof and sent a code to his driver. They rode the remaining journey in silence while Sheffield watched for any sign of Wilde to change his mind. Wilde only stared out the window into the darkness as they made their way to Madame Bellerose. When the carriage arrived, Wilde jumped out and waited for Sheffield to join him. When he didn't, Wilde stuck his head back inside the door.

"Not going to join me tonight, old chap?"

"No, I'm afraid now that I have made my decision to find a bride, I will no longer be visiting these establishments. I would hate to bring disgrace to any lady in my immediate acquaintance."

"Very proper of you, Sheffield. I guess more fun for me. I will convey Belle your regards. She will be most disappointed with your absence. You are her favorite."

Sheffield nodded his head to Wilde. "Enjoy the rest of your evening."

Wilde nodded his head back, then turned to enter the establishment hidden in the shadows. To any other observer, the townhome was a quiet house tucked into the corner of a respected area of Covent Garden. While the Gardens were known to host many houses of ill repute, this house hid the underbelly of the dark society of London. Only the elitist of the ton held knowledge of Madame Bellerose. To be allowed entry, a member of the club must sponsor your entrance. Wilde gained his access through Sheffield.

Upon reaching the door, he gave the secret knock to gain access to the pleasures of sin. Madame Bellerose only hired the most elegant women to satisfy her clientele. All the girls were required regular physician exams paid for by the Madame. Her girls never carried diseases or became pregnant. If they did, Belle removed them from service. Then she would make the gentlemen who ruined them provide money for the girl to move and to set her up for the rest of her life. This was not your normal brothel, nor were the girls your normal prostitutes. They were skilled at the highest levels of experience. The acts they could do with their mouths and hands made even Wilde blush.

As he handed off his hat and cane to the doorman, Belle glided along the hallway to greet him. She was grace and naughty wrapped tightly in a creation of red. The red dress hugged her figure and displayed her charms to perfection. Her breasts poured out of her gown, enough to tease a gentleman toward temptation with no imagination needed. The rest of her body spilled into her gown and displayed her generous curves. While many gentlemen wished to sample the charms of Madame Bellerose, her private services were not for sale. Oh, many men had tried, but they were removed from her club. She made an exception for Wilde though, but he only got to taste, never the full course. On many nights, they talked late into the night over a few glasses of wine. He would then charm her into a few kisses and light petting. But she would soon call a halt and send him off with her favorite girl for the night. Belle wasn't a conquest of his, but a very good friend. Maybe she could help him forget about the lovely lady he'd met earlier that evening.

"Oh, my darling Wilde. I am ecstatic to see a friendly face this evening. Are you alone, or will Sheffield be joining you?" she inquired as she wrapped her arm though his and pressed her body against him. Her breasts brushed across his arm.

"I am sorry to say Belle, that Sheffield will not be joining us this evening or any evening in the future. He sends his regards."

Belle stopped them in their tracks as her mouth hung open in surprise. He chuckled and tipped her mouth closed. The shock apparent on her face swiftly turned to disappointment, and then to sadness. He guided her into her private parlor and closed the door behind them. He settled her on the couch and continued to her liquor cart. Wilde poured them both a generous glass of whiskey and sat next to her. He pressed the glass in her hand and clinked their glasses.

"Here's to friends and their demise, taking the dreaded steps toward holy matrimony." Wilde drank the liquid in one swallow.

"Do I hear a sense of envy in your sarcasm?" Belle asked as she sipped her whiskey.

"Me, envious of Sheffield's decision to marry?" he laughed. "Never."

Belle lounged on the sofa as she watched Wilde refill his glass. He quickly drank another glass, then filled it again. This time he took a sip as he wandered back to her. She decided he protested too much. When he rested next to her, she laid her head on his shoulder. Her fingers lightly caressed his thigh, and she felt him relax against her. It would go no further than this. She knew she was safe with Wilde. Safe from being violated. Safe from being pressured. Secure in herself. When she was lonely for the touch of a man, Wilde was her choice for companionship. His sweet kisses and the stroke of his fingers on her soul always settled her. Tonight, she would have to soothe his soul. She could tell something troubled him and would have to coax it from him with gentle persuasion.

"So, which lady has caught Sheffield's attention?"

"I don't know."

"What do you mean you don't know? You are his closest friend. Did he not confide in you?"

"He hasn't chosen yet, but he has set his eyes on a sweet new debutante."

"Who is she?"

"That I do not know, my dear. He refuses to provide me with her name."

Belle laughed. Of course, Sheffield was no dummy. He understood if he gave Wilde the name, he would lose. Wilde would charm the girl and leave Sheffield in the cold. The lady's gaze would never stray from Wilde. She must be special to draw the attention of these two gentlemen. But Sheffield was a fool and would lose either way. By not telling Wilde her name, it only drew out his intrigue. To win this lady's hand would be the chase of the season; but which gentleman would be the victor? While Sheffield presented himself as the most logical choice for any lady, her money was on Wilde. No lady had ever drawn the interest of this man to this degree. Belle recognized Wilde's curiosity toward this enigma of a woman.

"Why would he do that?"

"It does not matter; my hat is not in the race. She is welcome to Sheffield."

Wilde listened to the denial as it left his mouth and knew it was a lie. He wanted his hat in the race and realized it was pointless. She was not his usual flavor, and in the end, he didn't want the parson's noose around his neck. He knew he would only ruin her. However, as he sat there, he recalled their dance and the sensation of holding her in his arms. She was light as a feather, and her touch quickened his heartbeat. He shook his head. This was stupid. Sappy stupid. Any girl in this house could make his heart beat fast, among other things. She would be forgotten soon and never remembered again. Already the feel of Belle's touch on his thigh made him hard. He leaned back and closed his eyes as he allowed her touch to soothe him. He moaned as her hand slid higher. The picture of blue eyes gazing into his eyes while her fingers trembled as she—

He sat forward fast and his drink spilled across the front of his pants. Belle released a little yelp as he drenched her hand in liquor. She pulled her hand back and scooted away from the mess. Wilde uttered a string of curses as he reached into his pocket to pull out a handkerchief. He set the now empty glass on the table and reached for Belle's hand. He gently wiped her fingers and brought her hand to his lips for a kiss. The hand did not tremble, nor did he feel the spark he had felt earlier. He placed his lips to her smooth skin.

"I am sorry for my clumsiness, my dear."

Belle reached with her other hand and enclosed it around his. She witnessed the troubled look in his eyes and realized the young lady, whoever she may be, had already affected him more than he would allow himself to believe.

"I think you protest too much; the miss has affected you more than you realize."

"Nonsense. What do you say, will you allow me to enter your boudoir this evening?"

Belle released a husky laugh. What she wouldn't do to have Wilde in her bed. But she couldn't betray her love with another, no matter how much she desired him. It was best to allow him Eve for the evening and let him unleash his charm on another—before she decided to give into the temptation of his kisses.

Belle rose from the sofa and swayed to the door as she smiled at him over her shoulder. She winked at him as she opened the door. She whispered quietly to her doorman, then closed the door and waited. Wilde jumped to his feet to follow and stopped in front of her. Belle could tell he was eager with excitement; however, she would have to disappoint him. She placed her hands on his chest and then rose one hand to brush his hair away from his face.

"I am sorry, Wilde, but the answer is still no. Ned will escort you to Eve tonight. She is waiting for you now. When you are ready, I am available to talk. I might even be able to help you with your young miss."

Wilde laughed. "She is not my young miss, nor will she be. I thank you for your attention this evening. Now, I am off to enjoy the delectable Eve. Take care, Belle."

Belle stepped back as Wilde strolled up the stairs to Eve's room. She watched as he sauntered down the hall and charmed the other girls as they stood in their doorways. He paid attention to all of them and did not favor one over the other. This action alone was why they all loved him the most. It was a shame. She not only lost one customer tonight, but two.

Wilde realized why Belle wouldn't allow him to enter her bedroom. He only teased, but still it wasn't very nice of him. He understood the reason why she always declined his offers. Her heart belonged to another. It wasn't fair to her, but it was a life she decided to live. His thoughts turned from Belle to Eve as he opened the door to the room. Eve lounged on her divan, wearing nothing but sin. Her robe was transparent in the firelight and left nothing for his imagination. Her wild, sexy, long blonde hair tumbled around her shoulders in disarray. Eve's painted lips pouted at him and begged for his lips to kiss hers.

"I have been waiting all night for you, Wilde," Eve whined.

"I am sorry, baby. I had obligations to attend," Wilde explained as he shut the door.

Once inside, he undid his cravat and unbuttoned his shirt. He walked over to her and stroked his finger along the opening of her robe, touching her warm skin. When he reached the knot, his fingers dissolved the string and drew her robe apart. A sensuous woman lay before him, full breasts and curves any man would want to sample. He paused. One would think he stared at how gorgeous Eve looked, but the only vision that flashed before his eyes was of another. What would she look like spread out before him like this? Her innocence would only be an added attraction. Damn.

Wilde closed Eve's robe and walked over to the chair where he threw his coat and cravat. He slid on his coat and put his tie in his pocket. He raked his hands through his hair and released a huge sigh. Belle was correct; he did want the chit. It was fifty different ways wrong, but it all felt so right. But for now, he needed to turn around and soothe Eve's feelings. He couldn't go through with this. It would not be fair to his conquest if he weren't truly honorable to her. For he realized Sheffield would be, as well as any other gent who courted her. Oh, he didn't imagine happily ever after with her, but a little fun along the way never hurt anybody.

When he turned around, he needed to duck as a pillow flew near his head. Eve stood in rage at his rejection. She looked for something else to hit him with—something more hurtful than a pillow. When she lifted a vase, Wilde moved to her side in an instant. He pried the vase from her hands and set it back on the table. He enclosed her in his arms and held her as her anger settled. Wilde pulled away, gently tipped her head, and placed a kiss on her cheek.

"You look stunning tonight, beautiful Eve."

"Not enough for your attention."

"It is not you, but me. I forgot an engagement I am expected at. I forgot I was to escort my sister home from a ball. Please forgive me, Eve. I promise, I will make amends to you." The lie slipped easily from his lips. There was no ball, let alone a sister to escort.

"Promise?"

"I promise. Now be a dear and forgive my insensitive nature."

She pouted her forgiveness as she settled back on the divan. Since, he didn't want to leave her disappointed in him, he leaned over and took her lips in a kiss. It was a kiss to show her how desirable he found her. His lips dominated her into sighs. He pulled back reluctantly and called himself a sucker. He never let another woman dictate his carnal urges. Maybe he should spend the night with Eve. Maybe then he could remove the debutante from his thoughts. When he bent over to kiss Eve again, her heavy perfume invaded his senses. Eve's musky scent overpowered him as his memory recalled the scent of lilies, and his mystery lady's huge eyes stopped him in his tracks. He drew away and decided to leave before he did anything he would regret.

Wilde left Eve's room and wandered outside. Once outside, he hailed a hackney and directed the driver toward his club. There he could get rip-roaring drunk and erase the look of sweet innocence from his mind. He would drink enough spirits to stop himself from acting all sorts of a fool. Wilde would drink the touch of her fingers under his away. He hoped anyhow.

~~~~~~

Sidney stayed awake past midnight recording her notes. She collected more data from the ball than she expected. It started as a little experiment, but her thoughts turned into the realization of making this a full thesis. Everything from a gentlemen's reaction to a lovely face who was dressed to perfection, to the competitive spirit gentlemen displayed for a lady's hand. Those were only a few examples compared to what she observed. There were also her reactions to the evening's festivities. From her dancing to her conversations with her three primary subjects. Each interaction held different experiences from the other, but they each held a spark of attraction of some sort. One thing more than apparent was each gentleman's reaction to her appearance. Each one of them scrutinized her bodily form from the top of her head to the tips of her toes—more than once.

Never one to be shallow, Sidney had to appreciate their gazes. While she never cared if a gentleman thought she was attractive, she did enjoy having her ego stroked. Their compliments made her feel special. Now she began to understand how simple girls turned crazy at a few words of flattery. When someone comments on your display of beauty, it gives confidence in yourself. This experiment would be an eye opener for Sidney in more ways than one.

A single look remained locked in her mind more than the others. It was his gaze that touched deep into her soul. When their eyes met as he kissed her hand good-bye, they spoke of a connection she was unclear on but wanted to discover the unspoken. She remembered how her hand trembled under his and how disappointed she became when he left her, not once glancing back.

Sidney rose from her desk of scattered papers and moved to her bed. Marquess Noah Wildeburg. Wilde. The lone wolf of the English ton who shied away from debutantes. If he dallied with them, it was only to leave them in ruin. No good ever came from any lady who fell into Wildeburg's trap of charms. He rescued her toes and danced with her. He sought her out, amongst all others. All the other gentlemen from the ball faded as she recalled word for word of their exchange. As her eyes drifted shut, her mind faded away to dream of his touch.

Chapter Four

The blinding sun streaming in through the windows and the covers being dragged away from her curled form interrupted Sidney the next morning from a deep sleep. If that wasn't bad enough, the bustle of servants invaded her room with water for a bath. Then her mother shouted instructions to her maid about her attire for the day. Sidney moaned and pulled the blanket back over her head as she tried to block out their invasion. However, her mother had other plans for her.

"It is time to rise, Sidney. We need to prepare you for afternoon calls. Our house is already full of flowers this morning. You were a hit last evening. The parlor will be packed with beaus dancing attendance on you. Oh, the excitement. Your poor father has locked himself in his study with instructions not to be disturbed."

Sidney pulled the covers past her eyes as she watched the flurry of her mother conferring with Rose, her maid. Each of them tossed dresses from her wardrobe to the side as they tried to find the right day dress that would complement her complexion, which would be difficult because Sidney usually chose more predictable and dependable garments to wear, not the flattering type.

"She has nothing, Lady Hartridge. Whatever shall we do? The gentlemen will run when they see her in these dresses."

"Yes, all rags, every last one. Well it is a splendid thing Sidney is the same size as Sophia Turlington. I sent a missive asking Sophia to loan Sidney a few dresses until we can get her to the modiste. She should arrive shortly with them. For now, Sidney shall bathe, and you can style her hair before her callers appear."

Sidney sighed. "Is all this necessary, Mama?"

"Yes, darling. The duke shall arrive, so you must be your best dressed for him above all others."

"How do you know the duke will call today? He said nothing to the contrary after our dance."

"But that is proof right there. He danced with you, therefore he will call on you today, not your father."

"Mama, I am sure Sheffield dances with many girls and does not visit them the next day."

"Very true, but then again you are not any ordinary girl. When you caught his eye last night, he couldn't take his gaze off you. Even your Papa remarked on Sheffield's interest in you."

Sidney half listened to her mother prattling on about the duke's regard for her, as well as the other gentlemen she danced with last night. She didn't have time for this interruption today. She needed to document the rest of her data and prepare for the next stage of her experiment. However, afternoon tea with a variety of male suitors calling on her would be an excellent opportunity to gather more data, especially if her main subjects were all present. Yes, this was a grand idea.

As she rose from bed, she made her way over to her desk to clear her work from the night before. If her mother or Rose caught wind of her research, it would be over before it even started.

She gathered the papers and slid them into the top drawer. When she glanced toward her mother and Rose, she noticed they were still going through her wardrobe, taking note of which pieces to keep. Since they paid her no attention, she locked the drawer and hid the key in her secret hiding place. Sidney sat in her chair as she waited for directions. She realized it was pointless to argue with her mother, nor did she want to. Her mother's excitement over Sidney finally being taken noticed of caused Sidney to remain quiet. She did not want to steal the joy of this moment away from her.

The greatest wish for any mother of the ton was for a duke to notice their daughter—not only the mothers but the fathers too. If a duke called upon a young lady, then there was never a worry the young girl would marry. The young lady didn't necessarily have to marry the duke. She could marry anybody. Her chances for marriage greatly increased simply because of the attention the duke paid her. All the gentlemen would compete for her hand, if only to brag that they had snagged her from a duke.

Before long, there was a bustle of activity outside her bedroom door. Lady Turlington breezed into her bedchamber, with Sophia trailing in on her tail. Phee rolled her eyes as their mothers embraced each other, gushing with excitement at Sidney's good fortune. As Sidney and Sophia were best friends, so were their mothers. When the two older women came together, they were a force to be reckoned with. It was yet another reason why Sidney wouldn't be able to back out of her experiment. Lady Turlington would make it her mission for Sidney to wed. If Sidney secured a grand match, then she could pave the way for Phee to make one too. While Sidney had no intention of getting married, she couldn't bring herself to halt their fun. In the end, Sidney knew she wouldn't be a bride, but she would deal with that later.

Phee wandered to her side and leaned against the desk. She gave Sidney the *what have you gotten yourself into* stare.

"I told you this wasn't a good idea," Phee whispered.

"Nonsense. This is working out better than I had planned."

"How so? You are about to be called on today by London's most eligible bachelors."

"I know. It's perfect. What better way to do my research than by having them come to me instead of me searching them out?"

"This is crazy, Sid. You will get caught, and then you will have to marry one of them."

"You worry too much, Phee. I have it all under control. There is so much to tell you too. I wish we were alone."

"That will be impossible, unless you can get our mothers' attention directed elsewhere."

"I have an idea."

Sidney wandered near the bed, where the two women discussed which of Sophia's dresses they could alter for Sidney to wear this afternoon. She trailed her fingers over the soft material. The silk felt soft against her fingertips. She wondered how it would slide against her skin, compared to her usual woolen dresses. A light blue dress, with lace for trim, caught her eye. Her hand hovered over the creation as she glanced at Phee. She sent her friend a silent message, asking if she could borrow the dress and if it would be a good choice. Their silent exchanges made their friendship perfect. They understood each other so well, they finished each other's thoughts. Phee smiled her approval and nodded her head at Sidney's choice. Sidney lifted the dress off the bed and turned toward her mother.

"Mama, will this dress do? I think I heard some girls gossiping last night that the duke's favorite color is blue."

Both mothers gasped at this piece of news. She heard Phee choke back a laugh at her lie. Her mother directed Rose on the alterations while Lady Turlington offered her own suggestions.

"Why, Sidney, this dress will look marvelous on you. The blue washes Sophia's color out. We must hurry, Franny, if we are to get this dress done in time." Lady Turlington gathered the dress from Sidney's grasp and hurried Lady Hartridge out the door.

"Yes, Cora, we must rush to prepare this gown. Come, Rose, we must have all the hands we can get," Lady Hartridge agreed as they rushed out of the bedroom. As soon as she left, she popped back into the room. "Now, Sidney please stay out of trouble until we return. Can you and Sophia visit in your room?"

"Yes, Mama. We will wait for your return here. We must compare notes about the ball."

"Notes? You aren't—"

"No, Mama, of course not. I meant gossip. Old habits die hard."

Her mother gave her a doubtful stare. Sidney could tell her mother wanted to question her further, but Lady Turlington called for her attention. With a frown, she reluctantly followed her friend. Sidney would have to work on her terminology better, or else someone would catch onto her lies. She glanced over at Phee to receive a look that indicated that was a close call. Sidney moved to the door, shutting it against any listening ears. She moved over to the window and motioned for Phee to join her on the window seat. When Phee rested next to her, Sidney reached for her hand and shifted toward her to share her data.

"I gathered so much research, I don't even know where to begin," Sidney laughed.

"First, I must tell you who you danced with before the Duke of Sheffield. It was No—"

"Noah Wildeburg," Sidney finished.

Sophia pulled away with a look of astonishment. "How can you sit there calmly? He is the worst scoundrel of the ton."

"And he is perfect for my experiment. I could not have gotten any luckier."

"Sidney, he will ruin you. You must not pursue him in your theory."

"Oh, I won't be pursuing him. He will be pursuing me."

"What makes you think he will seek your company?"

"He will chase after me out of competition. There was another factor I had not considered before, until I was caught between Wildeburg and Sheffield. There was a sense of competitiveness between the two."

"It spells trouble. I thought you already had a marquess picked out."

"Yes, Holdenburg, but I have scratched him. I danced with him at the ball, and he was a total bore. He couldn't see past himself or a deck of cards enough for me to entice him. No, Wildeburg will be a much better choice. Mark my words, Phee, he is interested."

"How can you be so sure? He doesn't mess with many debutantes, let alone the wallflowers."

"Well I'm not a wallflower anymore, am I? Plus, I sensed a connection with him last night."

"What kind of connection?"

"There was a spark when he held my hand, and his eyes turned heavy with…" Sidney became lost in her thoughts as she remembered her moment with Wildeburg.

"Sidney?" Sophia watched as her friend turned dreamy. This was not the Sidney she knew. Wildeburg left more of an impact on Sidney than she realized.

"Mmm, yes? Well … You know … That is…" Sidney mumbled as she rose and walked to her desk. She drew out her notes and turned to Phee, "Here are my notes from the ball." She handed them over for her friend to read.

"Don't think for one minute I don't recognize how Wildeburg has affected you more than you are saying. On top of that, Rory is suspicious of your behavior, and he will not be easy to detour."

"I am unused to the charms of a rogue, and it threw me off balance. However, I have my head together this morning, and I understand how focused I need to be around these gentlemen. I will take care of Rory. I decided he shall play a part in this experiment too. I didn't realize I could draw his interest, but he looked upon me differently too. Another aspect to my research: how to entice a friend into kissing me."

"You are playing with fire, and you will get burned."

"Mmm, funny. Rory said almost the exact same thing when we danced."

"I guess there is no changing your mind?" Phee asked.

Sidney released a laugh, "Absolutely not. The fun has yet to begin."

Sophia realized her friend wouldn't stop in her pursuit of the knowledge of a gentlemen's behavior towards a lady who interested him. So, she must follow Sidney and make sure she stayed out of as much trouble as she could. When Sidney decided to accomplish a goal, there was no stopping her until she reached the end. Sophia only hoped Sidney avoided a scandal. Because from where she sat, she looked to be heading toward one.

Sidney regarded Sophia as she read through her notes. She realized her friend worried about her getting into trouble. However, she had developed a plan to avoid any sort of scandal. She didn't tell her the most important aspect of her research: to find them soul mates. Sidney believed there was somebody special out there for everybody, and they only needed to find each other. That was the sentimental side of her that was in opposition to her scientific mind. She was a romantic at heart. While she studied the tomes of scientific nature and human behavior with her father, she secretly read romantic novels late into the night. Nobody knew about her secret habit, not even Phee. They shared everything, but this one secret Sidney kept to herself. She didn't understand why, because Phee would never judge her for it. She would want to trade novels back and forth. Sidney felt that if she understood how the male species courted, she could find them their mates. She already knew the traits of Sophia and herself, and now all she needed to discover were the traits of the gentlemen who would be compatible with them. Her three subjects were complete opposites from each other and would be perfect to study. Set aside the attraction toward one of the gentlemen, and she would be successful in this endeavor.

"If I read this correctly, you are saying the number one thing a gentleman will pursue a lady for is her looks. For starters, he will ask her to dance if she is pleasing to the eye by how attractive she is dressed."

"Yes, all the gentlemen proved the theory at the ball. Sheffield most of all."

"How so?"

Sidney wandered around her room, keeping her face shielded from Phee. She didn't want her friend to notice her hurt feelings. "He didn't even recognize who I was. He had to ask me what my name was while we danced."

"Of all the arrogant, pompous fools."

Sidney laughed at the description of Alexander Langley, the Duke of Sheffield. Phee's support soothed her hurt thoughts. "Yes, he is at that. However, he apologized, and we shared a lovely dance. Only now I'm afraid Mama has it in her head that he will offer for me. The duke is the last man I want or need."

"No, you do not need to be saddled with somebody who thinks he is above all else. I will help discourage him from you after you have collected your data from him. He is most definitely not your type."

"None of them are my type, Phee. I am only using them for research. Nothing else. I will not marry any of these gentlemen."

"Oh, I never thought this day would come. My Sidney getting married. Did you hear, Cora, she will marry one of these gentlemen?" Lady Hartridge bragged as she overheard Sidney's comment when they returned to the room.

"Well, of course, she will, Franny. Why else are we dressing her for success? Now we must hurry. Your parlor is filling up fast. We cannot keep those young bucks waiting, or else they will move on to greener pastures."

Sidney glanced at Phee for help. Phee shook her head with a twist to her lips, relaying the message of *you got yourself in this mess and I cannot help you where our mothers are concerned.* Sidney sighed in defeat and allowed them to guide her along in making herself presentable for all the beaus awaiting her below.

~~~~~

Sheffield stood near the windows in the overcrowded parlor, waiting for Sidney Hartridge to make her appearance. As his gaze scanned the other occupants of the room, he concluded he would have competition for her hand unless he stated his intentions to her, and everybody present, when she entered. Many of the young chaps would be too frightened to challenge him. Those who were not young wouldn't want to jeopardize any power they might hold in Parliament. He was always the deciding vote on many issues, and they would not want to lose his vote over a mere girl. One who was Sidney Hartridge at that. He lifted his cup and took a swallow of the lukewarm brew. He grimaced. He hated the taste of tea, but he did not wish to offend his hostess, who kept glancing in his direction. Lady Hartridge gave herself away when she twisted her hands in her lap as her head turned toward the door at each new entry, to no avail. Her daughter had not shown herself.

"I'm surprised to see you here, and waiting so patiently I might add," a voice spoke near his shoulder.

"Why should that surprise you? I have visited here many times in the past, especially with Lady Sidney," Sheffield replied.

"Ah, but usually it is in her father's study, and only because she inserted herself in your arguments to refute your viewpoint. Not in her mother's parlor waiting to pay attendance on her."

"Yes, well I wanted to thank her for a lovely dance and to pay my respects to her mother before I spoke with Lord Hartridge. It would be a display of poor manners if I were to leave before the miss appeared. Even though her rudeness would be the perfect excuse for me to leave this show. I could say the same to you, Lord Beckwith."

"Oh, I enjoy tea with the family frequently."

"Yes, you seem to favor the chit in our debates. Your crush is more than obvious. It would appear you waited too long and have a bit of competition now."

"She has never been a crush, only a close friend. Are you declaring your pursuit of her, Sheffield?"

"Mmm, I might be. If Lady Sidney is up to par, that is. Excuse me. It seems as if the lady has finally arrived." Sheffield left Beckwith fuming at his offhand remark.

Sophia came up behind Rory in a fit of anger. "Up to par? He should be so lucky. Why that conceited—"

"Calm down, Phee. He is not worth your frustration."

"He laid down an insult against our friend," argued Phee.

"Yes, but he is a pompous arse, and Sidney will not grant him the time of day. Look now, she barely acknowledges his presence," laughed Rory.

They stared as Sheffield made his appearance known to Sidney, who in return thanked him for visiting and continued onto the next gentleman, offering her gratitude. She treated Sheffield like any other caller, not paying him any more attention just because he was a duke. It seemed to frustrate Sheffield that she didn't bow down before him. Sidney continued through the parlor, talking to each gentleman before she sat next to her mother. She laughed at their attempts at humor and blushed at their compliments. All the while, the duke stood at the doorway with a dumfounded expression on his face, which couldn't have pleased her friends more.

Sheffield stood in anger at the small rebuff. All he needed to do was to leave without acknowledging her, and this would be the final time their parlor filled to capacity. He could ruin her with one action. As he spun to leave, he noticed Beckwith move to her side to greet her. He halted as he observed how much she enjoyed receiving the man. Her face lit with delight as her eyes twinkled in a teasing manner. It was then that Sheffield realized he wanted her to gaze upon him that way—him alone. Instead of leaving, he strode toward them and bowed before her like a humbled servant. He nudged Beckwith out of the way as he grabbed for her gloved hand. As he lifted her hand to his lips, he placed a soft kiss on her fingers. He heard her gasp and felt her tremble.

"I thank you for the lovely tea, Lady Sidney."

"You are welcome, Your Grace. I apologize for my swift greeting, but Mama always instilled in me to be gracious to every guest, no matter their rank. Because if somebody calls on you in kindness, then you must extend them the same grace."

He lightly squeezed her fingers as he turned to her mother and bowed his head. "Your mother has groomed you with the worthiness of manners. My respect Lady Hartridge, for raising such a delightful young lady."

Sidney tried not to roll her eyes at his pompous charm. She noticed the change in his behavior after Rory greeted her. He went from being furious at her rebuff to possessive when another male paid her attention. He now staked his claim and let every gentleman present understand it. By praising her mother, it all but guaranteed him as a favorite with her parents. She noticed the effect of his attentions on her mother. Her mother beamed with pride from the courtesy the duke paid them. She needed to end this and send Sheffield on his way, so she could focus on the less trivial men of her research. The other gentlemen here would provide groundwork, and she needed to analyze their reactions. Plus, the warmth of his hand holding hers disturbed her. His thumb had caressed the back of her fingers where nobody could see. She felt warm from his added devotion, sighing from his touch. His eyes trapped hers to let her know he heard and shot her a smirk filled with the assurance of his chase.

"Will you accompany me on a ride through Hyde Park tomorrow morning?" Sheffield asked Sidney.

Sidney nodded her head in acceptance, much to the groans of the other gentlemen present. She found it difficult to speak while he held her hand. He never displayed his charm to her before, so she was unprepared for the full assault. The thing Sidney was certain of was the level of his charisma. She didn't think it was at his maximum, but it soon would be.

"Excellent. I will arrive at ten o'clock." He let his fingers slide from hers and smiled as he took his leave.

Sidney heard Rory *humph* behind her and turned to discover why. However, before she could ask, he trailed out of the room behind Sheffield. When her eyes sought Phee, it was to find her friend glaring at the men who left. Which one, Sidney was unsure of, but would inquire on their walk. Soon a few more gentlemen departed. She needed to keep the remaining from leaving or else she would gather no data. To do that, she would have to rely on the false charms young maidens used to be courted upon. She cringed at her deceptive behavior, but it was the only way. Sidney played at the simpering female who gushed with delight on being called upon by so many worthy gentlemen. The sad part of it all was that they fell for it— every giggle, "Oh my," and blush she forced out.

~~~~~~

Noah Wildeburg lounged in the seat of his unmarked carriage. He had waited for Sheffield to leave Hartridge's residence for two hours. His suspicion rose when he noticed Lord Hartridge leave an hour ago, but still Sheffield remained. Why did he stay inside? When Smith knocked on top of the carriage, sending him a signal, Wilde moved to the window to watch Sheffield depart from the townhome. He walked with a confident gait, whistling. Lord Roderick Beckwith followed him out of the house in anger. Wilde thought there would be a confrontation, but Beckwith strode off in the opposite direction. What was that all about? Was this where the mystery girl resided? Impossible, as Hartridge only had one daughter. A mousy, opinionated bluestocking from how Sheffield described the chit. Somebody his friend would never be interested in, let alone want to wed. Soon the stoop filled as more gentlemen left the residence. Noah sent a signal for Smith to wait. He would catch up with Sheffield later at the club. The mystery inside Hartridge's home sparked his curiosity.

He wouldn't have long to wait. The door opened with two young misses stepping outdoors. It was her. There was no mistake about it. He knew if he followed Sheffield today, it would lead him to discover her identity. While he still didn't know her name, he knew where to find her. There was no mistaking the beauty he met the evening before. He felt his heart beat faster at the mere sight of her. This feeling wouldn't do, but he must explore the attraction. The two young ladies took off walking along the sidewalk, their heads bent together, whispering secrets to one another. Wilde sent a knock to Smith and ordered the man to follow at a discreet distance.

Wilde's carriage followed them for a couple of blocks, where her friend hugged her and entered a townhome. His mystery lady continued her stroll along the street toward a park nearby. Once she entered the park, Wilde lost sight of her. He yelled for Smith to stop the carriage and gave him instructions to return home. Wilde then entered the park, searching for any sign of her. He located her on a bench near the pond as she read from a book. Her legs were drawn underneath her, and she was lost deep in concentration. Her gloveless fingers turned each page slowly as she devoured the words. She mouthed the words as she read them. He leaned against the tree, watching her. He didn't quite understand what it was about her that drew him to her. Before he realized it, he stood before her, blocking the sun. She glanced from the book as a shadow fell over her. When her gaze rose to him, she closed her book and slid it under her skirts, hiding the book from his view.

"I did not mean to startle you. I only wished to say hello."

"You did not startle me. Hello."

"Hello." He smiled at her. "Do you mind if I sit?"

Sidney unwound her legs and scooted to the edge of the bench, brushing her skirt aside. "Please do."

Wilde settled on the other end of the bench a respectable distance away and turned toward her. He regarded her nervousness and wanted to put her at ease. He realized he would need to move slowly with this one, which he was fine with. All the sweeter when he succeeded. A blush graced her cheeks at his stare, and he admired the becoming color on her.

"It is a lovely afternoon for the park," he started the conversation.

"Yes."

"Especially for reading."

Her cheeks became red as she answered, "Yes."

"May I inquire as to what you are reading?"

"Oh, nothing of importance." Sidney felt her face grow redder. The last thing she needed was for Noah Wildeburg to catch a glimpse of her novel. If he saw her romance book, he would spread word to his friends, mainly Sheffield, and she could never voice her arguments in her father's discussions again. Nobody would take her seriously. She inched the book under her skirts more.

"No matter. I find reading a bore. I would much rather act out life experiences than read about them," he informed her as he slid closer to her on the bench. He glanced around and took note of the empty park. It was only the two of them in this moment in time. An instance to be short-lived, so he wished to make the most of it. That is, if he wanted to make any kind of impact on her above all her other suitors.

He reached out to tuck a loose curl around her ear. His fingers lightly traced behind her ear as he drew his hand away. He listened to her sharp intake of breath as she turned her head toward him. Their gazes locked with one another, neither one of them glancing away. Locked in a moment he wished for and was being granted. She reached to touch where his hand briefly touched and lingered. He gulped as her eyes darkened to a midnight blue as they did the night before. Shaking himself from her trance, he cleared his throat.

"I am sorry to say I am at a loss. I do not know your name."

Sidney felt a sense of déjà vu. The only difference was that he wasn't the same man who spoke those same words from the night before. Was she normally that undesirable? Sidney found it hard to believe mere clothes and a fancy coiffure transformed people's reactions to you. She must be wrong in her theory, for that was what happened to her. True, she usually wore glasses and tied her hair in a mere bun for convenience. Her dresses were always quality dresses designed from affordable material. No, they were not in pretty colors with lace and tulle adorning them. They were practical dresses while she worked alongside her father on his research. Still, it stung that nobody had taken notice of her before.

"Sidney Hartridge."

"Are you a niece to Lord Hartridge? New to town, are you?"

"No, My Lord, I am his daughter."

"Impossible, why Sheffield always said—" Wilde stopped himself, for he did not want to offend the chit.

"The Duke of Sheffield always said what, exactly, about me?"

"Nothing, my dear girl, nothing."

Sidney laughed. "Oh, I doubt it was nothing. Please enlighten me."

From her tone of voice, Wilde knew the conversation was not going as he planned. How was he to know the beauty before him was Hartridge's daughter? The only comments he had overheard about her were her plain looks and her heavy-handed words. Never about what a beauty she was. Were they all blind, or had he missed something here?

"It would not be honorable of me to divulge a private conversation I held with a friend."

"Very well. I will ask him myself."

"You would not dare."

"Yes, actually I would. Tomorrow I think would be ideal."

"If you must know. Though I prefer not to hurt you."

"I insist you must. I do not desire to have a man court me who once thought badly of me."

"Is he courting you?" Wilde's voice held an edge to it.

"Mmm, I think so. He called on me today during afternoon tea and has requested my company for a ride with him in the park tomorrow. Yes, I believe he is beginning a courtship."

Wilde leaned against the bench, a twist to his mouth. He did not want to direct his anger at the young lady before him, but at Sheffield. The man had lied about his disinterest and had played him for a fool. Well two could play at this game. Far be it for Sheffield to have an easy time courting her. All is fair in love and war, they say.

"I would hate for any young lady to enter into a courtship under false pretenses."

"I am glad you see it my way. Now, what is the duke's opinion of me?"

Wilde hesitated on hurting the girl, but what he was about to speak only held truth. "He thought you were an opinionated mousy girl who needed to keep her viewpoints to herself and not pollute the rest of society with your thoughts."

"Humph."

"I warned you it was not pleasant."

"Oh, but he was only being honest, wasn't he?"

Tears came forth to Sidney's eyes as Wildeburg described Sheffield's opinion of her. Most of the tears were real, the others false. While it hurt her ego that a man of Sheffield's nature thought so lowly of her, the other part of her was realistic. Also, she witnessed for herself firsthand the duke's sentiments, and he made amends. However, she didn't want her other subject, Wildeburg to be aware of this. It was best to play along with whatever he decided his role would be. Plus, she must have left an impression on Sheffield, if he ever mentioned her at all. On some level, she held Sheffield's respect, that she was sure of. She made a mental note for tomorrow about voicing more opinionated thoughts with Sheffield.

"On the contrary. He was false. You are a beauty like no other, who has captured my attention and snared it in your web."

Sidney couldn't help but giggle at the outlandish compliment. "You, sir, are a flirt."

Wilde stood and bowed before her. "No flirt, My Lady. Marquess Noah Wildeburg at your service."

She waved him back to the bench. "Oh, I already know who you are, My Lord. Your reputation precedes itself."

"All false. Do not believe a word you have heard."

"Not all, I hope?" Sidney flirted back.

"No, not all," he whispered, replacing the loose curl behind her ear again.

Sidney inwardly sighed at his touch as she realized the flirtation was moving too fast. She rose swiftly and backed away from the bench.

"I must leave. I promised Father I would help him this afternoon."

Wilde stood, "I hope I did not hurt your feelings too badly concerning Sheffield."

"You only spoke the truth, and that is all I can ever ask of any gentleman. You see, he must respect me if he ponders over my comments. If my viewpoints were lacking, then he would never have remembered them. So, he must hold me in a higher esteem than you think. As for the mousy part, well it was true. I dressed plainly and wore glasses. Since, I made promises to my mother to land a groom this season, I have taken more care with my appearance. A gentleman would want to find his wife desirable, would he not?"

He stood speechless at her reaction. His plan to diminish Sheffield's courtship had backfired. Not only that, her declaration of a search for a groom had his mind screaming, *Run away*. The last thing he needed was to be caught. How did he answer such a loaded question as that? Desirable, her? She was beyond the word desirable. She was an enchantress. *Run, Wilde, run and don't look back.*

"No man will ever have that trouble with you, my dear. Since Sheffield is taking you for a ride tomorrow, would you mind very much if I walked you home? For your own protection, of course. I do not want anything to prevent your excursion tomorrow."

"I must decline. It wouldn't be proper for us to be seen without a chaperone. I have lingered too long as it is. I thank you for your kind offer and wish you a pleasant day."

Wilde nodded his good-bye. He granted her a smile of lazy indulgence as she looked over her shoulder at him. Lady Sidney hurried her pace along the path as she left the park. He sighed as he sat back down. However, the book she left uprooted his balance on the bench. He pulled it from under his leg and stared at the title. The little minx. She was a romantic at heart. It was something she tried to hide, not only from him, but from everybody else, he suspected. His chances to win her just improved. As he stood, he slid the book inside his pocket. Wilde whistled a favorite tune as he left the park, making his way home. It seemed he would not spend his afternoon at the club, after all. Instead he had a book to read.

Chapter Five

Alex followed the voices down the hallway. Lord Hartridge's butler Emerson informed him he was to join them in the dining room as they finished their breakfast. As he stood outside the room, he tried to keep a tight rein on his annoyance. His title should have given the butler a reason to announce his presence. Instead, he wandered the unorthodox household in his search for the Hartridge family. When he came upon them, he found them in their normal chaotic routine. Everybody talked at once, each discussing a different topic. How anybody followed the conversations, he held no clue. He would have to grin and bear it while he courted Lady Sidney. Once he established her in his own household, his life would return to normal.

As he stood in the doorway clearing his throat, the room quieted a bit. Once they noticed him, Lady Hartridge motioned for the servants to grab him a chair. Lord Hartridge bellowed out a greeting while the rest of the family went on with their conversations, which seemed more like arguments. Alex searched the room for Lady Sidney, to draw her away for their ride, when he noticed her head bent in a whispered discussion with Lord Beckwith. She paid him no attention, ignoring his appearance while she sipped her tea and buttered a croissant. Did she also ignore the look Beckwith bestowed her with? Surely, she was not immune to his glances. When she touched the other gentleman's hand, Alex realized she wasn't indifferent to his stares. His annoyance grew to anger the longer she didn't direct her attention toward him.

Rory wanted to chuckle at Sheffield's dilemma but didn't want to make life difficult for Lord Hartridge, or Sidney for that matter. For whatever reason, Sheffield held an interest in his friend, and he wouldn't take this opportunity away from their family, even though a small part of him wished to prevent the courtship. There were small changes in Sid within the last few days that drew his interest. Subtle changes, but changes nonetheless that opened his eyes to her beauty. Oh, he always thought her lovely. He saw through her plainness ages ago. Their bond of friendship always meant more to him than his attraction to her. Now, he questioned if he should have courted Sidney before.

He noticed that her smile softened and her arguments held less of an edge. Perhaps it was because of her new dresses, or her auburn hair being curled, or the gentle touch of her hand upon his that left him in doubt. He knew he could not provide for her, and it was unfair to string her along. However, when she released a husky laugh at his joke, he asked himself why not. He stood as much of a chance as the haughty duke in the doorway. Oh, he noticed the man standing there glaring at them. He smiled at Sid as he lay his hand over hers. When he whispered to her on the presence of her date, she met his eyes with a silent message that twinkled her awareness of the duke. With the sparkle in her eyes and her dazzling smile capturing him, he forgot about her agenda and his doubts.

He sensed she pulled a prank of sorts and wanted to figure it out. Rory wanted to keep her out of trouble, but when she stared upon him as she did, his suspicions fled his mind. He transformed into an interested male and wanted to throw his hat into the competition. Rory decided right then and there he would also pursue Sidney. With the competition of Alexander

Langley, the Duke of Sheffield, it would be no easy feat, but it would be one he would endure for her hand. He brought her fingers to his lips and placed a kiss upon her knuckles. He offered her family his good-byes and thanked them for the morning meal. While he would bow out gracefully for now, he would return later to start his courtship.

"Good day, Sheffield. I hope you enjoy your ride." Rory tipped his head to the duke on his way down the hallway.

Sidney smiled as she watched the duke glare at Rory as he left. She could not believe her luck with this experiment. All the gentleman kept falling into her hands, giving her the research she needed without having to seek them out. She witnessed the anger Sheffield tried to hide under his cool demeanor, but she knew different. For she had seen his anger many times, mostly directed at her for her controversial viewpoints. He was definitely furious. She needed to soothe his ego, which was not something the old Sidney would do, but the Sidney who wanted results must appease him.

"Your Grace, you are earlier than I expected. Please, won't you join us for breakfast?"

"My Lady, I have already partaken in breakfast with my grandmother. I thought you would enjoy the ride before it rained for the day."

Sidney looked outside and noticed the sky clouding over. "An excellent idea. I shall fetch my bonnet and maid, then we can be on our way."

"No need for a maid. I trust Sheffield here with your care. I see no reason to drag Rose away for an uncomfortable ride, considering how she hates horses," Lord Hartridge instructed.

"If you're sure, Papa. I will return shortly, Your Grace."

"I am at your convenience, My Lady," Sheffield replied, his temper calmed at her behavior. She seemed to want to please him.

Sheffield made small talk with her father while her mother ushered the younger children to the nursery for their studies. When Lady Sidney returned, she went to her father's side, kissed him on the cheek, and wished him a pleasant day. At that moment, Alex took full notice of her. Her relaxed attitude and affection toward her family highlighted her grace more fully. Her smile was genuine as it lit her face, displaying her beautiful features. It surprised him that he had never noticed her charms before. She put on no airs. This was her true self. Captured in staring at her beauty, she caught him unaware as she stood before him, waiting patiently for his attention. Only when she spoke did he notice the smug glint in her eyes, which she masked with serene indifference. When she gifted him with an innocent smile, he dispelled any hidden agenda. He must have imagined the look.

"I will have her back within an hour," Sheffield addressed Lord Hartridge.

"Whenever, Sheffield." Lord Hartridge waved them off as he engrossed himself in a newspaper article.

Sidney laughed as her Papa ignored them. She clutched Sheffield's arm and guided him outside. When they stood on the sidewalk, she looked above to notice that the sky had darkened. Not wanting to lose out on this opportunity to spend time alone with the duke, she continued onto his curricle. Once she reached the vehicle, Sheffield helped her to sit on the high seat. As she spread out her skirts, Sheffield climbed upon the rig, taking the leads. With a command to his horses, they soon hurried on their ride toward Hyde Park.

Neither one of them spoke, but smiled at each other when their eyes met. Conversation would have been difficult with their swift pace and the other carriages on the road, unless, they wanted to shout. Soon Sheffield had them trotting along Rotten Row at a much slower pace, negotiating his horses in position behind the other riders. He attempted to hold a private conversation many times, but the other visitors in the park interrupted him. When he tried for the fifth time to engage her with small talk, only to be disturbed again, he steered them off the path toward the exit. It would seem their ride in the park would end sooner than she thought. Instead, Sheffield turned toward a deserted path and pulled his curricle to a stop. He jumped off and came to her side, pulling her down into his arms before she questioned his intentions.

As she slid along his body, she became aware of his physical strength. Her hands gripped his arms so she wouldn't fall. His arms were tight, hard muscles. His jacket had no padding, unlike most men of the ton. He held her in his embrace for a few seconds longer than he should have, long enough for her to take notice that the rest of his body was as firm. It seemed the duke was no lightweight dandy, but kept himself in top physical condition. Another strong point in his favor. Sidney admired a man who took care of himself and didn't waste his time on the pursuits of the unsavory. She knew him to be a man with a scholarly mind but didn't realize he was one of the physical sorts too.

Her hands lingered on his forearms as her fingers traced the cords of his muscles through his coat. Unaware of what she did, Sidney became lost in her thoughts. She tried to understand the chemistry she felt toward Sheffield when she heard him groan. Startled, she raised her head to see that he watched her hands. They were no longer on his arms but had wandered to his chest and slid across his stomach. Aghast at herself, for her forward nature, she dragged her hands away and stepped out of his grasp. Flustered, she turned away and wandered farther along the wooded path. What had come over her? She pressed her gloved hands to her face to cool off the burn of embarrassment. Rushing away, she stumbled over a tree root, only to have her elbow grasped and righted again. Sheffield stopped her and spun her toward him.

"Sheffield …"

"Alex. Alexander, if you'd like the more proper form. Only my grandmother refers to me by my full name."

"Your Grace," she began again.

"Alex. Say it, Sidney," he stressed in the arrogant tone he used when he expected his demands to be granted.

"As I was saying, Sheffield," she tried for the third time, but he interrupted her when he drew her into his arms.

"I don't think you were saying anything as much as you were touching me, my dear," he whispered.

Alex reached to untie her bonnet from under her chin. He swept the hat off her head, and stray curls caressed her face as the wind blew around them. He reached to tuck them behind her ears, his fingers sliding over the silken tresses. When her hands had caressed his body, he felt comfort from her touch. It was no blinding attraction, but it felt nice. He could work with nice. Her hands were gentle, and he sensed her curiosity as she explored. He also realized her reaction embarrassed her, and he wanted to put her at ease. If, along the way, he were able to sample a taste of her, to finalize his decision on her being a perfect match for him, all the better. If her kiss satisfied him, then he could proceed with making arrangements with her father and call off the rest of her suitors.

He ran his fingers along her cheek and tipped her face under her chin with his knuckles, for their eyes to meet. He began to lower his head for a kiss when he heard his name being called in the distance. She heard it too, for her eyes grew large, and she tried to pull out of his embrace.

"We will finish this another time," he informed her before releasing her from his grasp.

"Sheffield, where are you, old chap?" shouted Wildeburg.

Sidney gasped when she heard the marquess shouting for Sheffield. She was beyond mortified. The Duke of Sheffield almost kissed her, and another one of her subjects nearly caught her in another man's embrace. Her research would have been over before it even began. While today she made more progress than the night of the ball, she still needed to gather more evidence. Not only were they almost caught, but they were alone in a wooded area. This would not have been good for her reputation if someone discovered them in each other's arms. She didn't wish to be saddled with the duke for a husband. While his touch provided comfort, it did not hold the kind of attraction she desired from the man who would be her husband. She wanted sparks and an undeniable attraction that would never be fulfilled no matter how hard they tried. No, Sheffield wasn't the gentleman for her.

Sheffield bent to lift her bonnet from the ground as he ushered Sidney into the clearing toward Wilde's voice. While he didn't wish to damage Sidney's reputation, he wanted Wilde to witness her in his presence. He needed for him to see they spent time alone together. With that, Wilde would realize he didn't stand a chance with her.

"Over here, Wilde. We were chasing Lady Sidney's bonnet. It became loose in the wind and needed rescuing." The lie easily slipped from his mouth.

"Who is this Lady Sidney? A delightful creature, I'd imagine, if you are off alone in the woods with her."

After his remark, Sidney's cheeks turned a brighter red. The wrong opinion had already begun to form about her. Furthermore, why did Lord Wildeburg pretend ignorance at the mention of her name? She supplied him with her name in the park yesterday. When she raised her head, she caught Wilde's eye, whereupon he sent a wink her way.

"Forgive me, Wilde. I thought you exchanged names when you danced at the ball. Let me introduce you to the lovely Lady Sidney Hartridge. Lady Sidney, my good friend, Marquess Noah Wildeburg."

Wilde bowed before her. "A pleasure, My Lady. Sheffield is expressing a tale, for I asked your name at the end of the ball. However, my good friend kept your identity a secret as he tried to beat me in the chase for your hand. I notice he has the lead, so I will have to make a move to pass him soon."

"As I remember, you were not interested in courting Lady Sidney, only trifling with her. As a friend of her father's, I felt it best to protect her from the likes of your attention."

"Trifling? Surely not, I would never want to damage a lady's reputation, especially one of Lady Sidney's high esteem."

"So, you are saying you wish to court her?" inquired Sheffield.

"Of course. Anything else would be too low for the lovely girl."

Sidney's head swished back and forth as she witnessed the exchange between the two gentlemen. While Sheffield's patience wore thin by the tone of his voice, Wildeburg's charm oozed out of him. Clearly these two weren't fighting over her, were they? The duke's eyes narrowed as he stepped toward Wildeburg, sending him a silent message. However, the marquess paid no heed to the threat, as he smiled and raised an eyebrow in achieving what he set to accomplish. She kept an eye on the two men as she tied the bonnet on her head. They appeared as two rams ready to lock horns, one tempting the other into a fight.

"While I am flattered from the attention of the two most sought after bachelors of the ton, I must insist that both of you withdraw your intentions. I would hate to come between two friends. Now, I enjoyed visiting with you again, Lord Wildeburg, but I must get home to Papa. I promised him help on his research today."

"Surely, your father can do without your help. I hoped you would take tea with my grandmother this afternoon," Sheffield said.

"Perhaps another time. My work with my father is very important to me."

"Yes, but once you marry, you cannot aid your father with his research."

"Why not?"

"Because, my dear girl, you must take care of your husband and your new home. Your schedule will not permit you to work," explained Sheffield.

"I don't consider it work, but a passion of mine."

"Well, your husband will be your new passion."

Of all the pompous attitudes, but then again, he was a duke, wasn't he? Another reason why he would not be a perfect groom for her or Sophia. If Phee were here, she and Sheffield would be in a full-blown argument. Of all the traits Sophia had no interest in, it was a demanding attitude. Sidney would scratch him off her list for both of them; however, he was good material for her research. Sidney needed to rein in her own temper and not comment on his opinions. In the end, it would not be worth it.

"I disagree, Sheffield. If any woman made her husband feel as loved as I'm sure Lady Sidney would, then what harm would it do for her to enjoy her own hobbies?" interrupted Wildeburg.

"Research is not a hobby," Sidney emphasized as she tried to make them understand how important her work was to her.

"All the more reason you need to chase your dreams," Wildeburg declared with a charming smile.

Sheffield noticed that he had lost ground with Lady Sidney. Wilde was displaying his full arsenal of charm. If he didn't backpedal soon, then he would lose her to a man who only set out to charm her in order to ruin her. There was nothing he could do that would prevent her ruination if Wilde desired her. No lady was immune to him, even one as practical as Lady Sidney. It was best if he kept quiet about his opinion on her research with her father for now. He would demand her devotion once she became his duchess. As his wife, she would have to obey his every command. If Wilde declared his intentions to court her, he would have to press his suit with her father as soon as possible. The time had come for him to return her home, where he would request a private word with Lord Hartridge.

"If you will excuse us, Wilde, I need to return Lady Sidney home." Sheffield offered his arm to Sidney, but Wilde blocked him.

"It was lovely to make your acquaintance again, My Lady. Until we meet again." Wilde lifted his hand to tuck a curl behind her ear. "Sorry. A stray curl came loose."

"Thank you, My Lord. The pleasure is all mine." She stepped around Wilde and lay her hand on Sheffield's arm, where he led them back to his curricle.

Once Sheffield took off, Sidney recalled their brief interchange. Lord Wildeburg surprised her with his remarks on her research. In truth, every one of his comments confused her. First, he pretended he didn't recognize her name, and second, his views on a woman's activities after marriage dumbfounded her. For those were not the views of most men— well, all men really. In society, women were meant to make a home for their husbands and to wait for their attentions. Her father was one of the few men who thought differently. Therefore, in her family, you were raised to follow your dreams. Her own mother did and taught her to do the same. It was the third and final action that flustered her the most.

When Wildeburg tucked the curl around her ear again, she felt a heat of attraction toward him. Luckily, Sheffield waited for her, or she would have done something as foolish as hold Wildeburg's hand to her face. Both men today performed the same action, yet she only felt a pull toward one. When Sheffield tucked her hair behind her ear, she felt nothing. Truth be told, she felt annoyed at his audacity to be so familiar with her, even though she had just caressed him. Still, he should have kept his hands to himself. But when Wildeburg completed the same action, his touch ignited a warmth in her that she craved more of. It reminded her of a scene from one of her romance novels. Sidney wanted to release a sigh at the romantic gesture but did not want Sheffield to question her. So, she rode in silence until they arrived at her townhome. As they walked to her front door, Sheffield stopped them on the stoop.

"If I may be so bold, I must warn you away from Lord Wildeburg. As his closest friend, I have witnessed firsthand the destruction he could cause a lovely young lady such as you."

"I thank you for your warning and for the delightful ride today, Your Grace. I will take your warning in stride. While I have seen none of the destruction you speak of, I will say he has been nothing but charming to me. Also, I am not some young miss who wears blinders to such charm. At least he is being honest with his intentions."

"As am I, Lady Sidney. I have showed my interest toward you and do not play you false."

Sidney laughed at the duke's confusion. "Mmm, a mousy know-it-all whose opinions need to be kept to herself. Does any of that sound familiar?"

Sheffield's look of shock said it all. He could not deny nor ask where she had heard such rubbish without betraying his previous descriptions of her appearance. But he had a clue where she had learned of his comments. Wildeburg. Who else would set to destroy his chances with Lady Sidney? While he could not slander Wilde without looking spiteful to the lady, he would give a word of warning to Lord Hartridge while he pushed his own agenda. Lord Hartridge was a sensible man and would take his word of warning to heart.

When the door opened, it saved Sheffield from having to answer her. Which was for the best, for she didn't want the duke to realize she talked with Wildeburg alone in the park yesterday. He would inform Papa. Her parents would never approve and would demand a chaperone be present wherever she went. She valued her privacy too much for that to happen. No, she needed to drop the subject. Her father appeared in the doorway, looking impatient for the delay to come inside the house. Sidney soothed her father with a kiss on the cheek and a promise to join him in his study after she changed. As she rushed up the stairs, she overheard the duke asking for a moment of her father's time. Her father agreed and ushered Sheffield into his study. Sidney raced to her room to change her clothes. She wanted to eavesdrop on their conversation. Too much happened this afternoon that could ruin her research.

After Rose helped change her dress, Sidney hurried to her father's study to find the room empty. She left the office and searched for her father, only for Emerson to inform her of his departure to his club. Sidney sighed and returned to sort through the piles on her father's desk. At least the duke was no longer present. Their conversation must have been a brief one at that. If they were to have discussed her, surely they would still be talking.

They must have discussed her father's latest research; the duke's investment weighed heavily in the truth of his discovery. Sheffield came across some documents that dated back to the sixteenth century and asked her father to prove them legit. That was all she understood of her father's latest project. It was one he kept hidden and would let nobody know the depth of the project, including her. It was strange, for he never kept anything private. He always shared his research with anyone who would listen. Sidney sat on the edge of the chair and opened drawers, looking for any clue to project. She realized she shouldn't snoop, but with Sheffield's courtship, she was curious on the contents of his papers.

As she opened the secret drawer in the desk, she glanced toward the door to make sure she was alone. Only she wasn't. Rory relaxed against the doorjamb. She silently slid the drawer closed, clicking the lock her father had carelessly left undone. While her opening the drawer was dishonest, anybody else's discovery of the papers would have been damaging to her father. She needed to search more to learn the story of what the research told. Sidney started to sort through the pile of papers on the desk, to appear innocent.

"Why, Rory, you gave me a fright."

"Snooping again, Sidney?"

"Of course not. I'm helping Papa with his paperwork."

"Mmm, in his private desk drawers?"

"Private desk drawers. What nonsense. Papa keeps nothing a secret. He is excited to share his findings with anybody who will listen."

Rory listened to Sidney as she rattled on to draw his attention elsewhere. But he knew better. He watched her as she snooped around, looking for Lord Hartridge's secret research. He didn't blame her curiosity, especially since Sheffield pursued her. As he observed her, he noticed the changes in her appearance. Once again, she dressed in a plain gown with her hair pulled in a braid, with glasses adorning her face. While he thought this was the image of his friend, the last few days proved different. Sidney had a mysterious side, and he had been unaware of it all these years. The woman before him stood false. The other woman beheld the true Sidney. While she appeared comfortable in both personas, the Sidney from earlier was more natural and meant to be. Her beauty was more than skin deep, though. Her mind held her true beauty. Her conversations captured any man's attention and changed their opinions to hers. Every man but the duke. He was the only one who did not appreciate her fully. He only hoped Sidney was not drawn into his dukedom the way everybody else was. But that wasn't possible. She was too practical.

"That he does, but we are both aware Sheffield has entrusted your father with classified documents. Have you had any luck finding them?"

Sidney settled into her father's comfy chair and scowled at Rory. "No, I haven't, and you are aware of that. Do you know where he has hidden them? Better yet, do you have information on their contents?"

Rory sat in the chair across the desk, picking lint off his suit jacket as he pretended indifference to her questions. While he was as curious as Sidney on the unknown documents, he would not draw her interest to them anymore. Lord Hartridge had stung his pride when he did not share his new discovery with him. The other part didn't want Sidney to become enamored of the Duke by these papers. If he fueled her interests, she would allow Sheffield to chase her, perhaps even catch her. For her own welfare, he must change the direction of her thoughts. Sidney wouldn't be satisfied with Sheffield for a husband. Of that, he was sure.

"No, I don't know where he locked them away. But from what I gather, they are only documents about some land the duke is interested in. Nothing too dramatic, I'm afraid."

"Darn. I hoped for something juicy to discover about Sheffield. I guess I will stop my search and help Papa clear his mess in here."

Sidney started stacking papers on her father's desk, putting them in the correct files. She realized her actions were useless, for Papa would spread the papers out all over again when he dove into his research. Even though her father kept his desk disorganized, he could tell you where he laid a document if he needed to locate it in a hurry. Her father performed all subjects of research for the Crown and for any peer of the realm. Anything from scientific research to antiquities discoveries. As long as Sidney could remember, she had helped him with his projects. His enthusiasm for each project drew her into their web of mystery. Her desire to understand the whys and hows always prompted her thirst for knowledge. It was in these quests Rory became a willing partner. He would be right by her side until the end when they discovered the answers to their questions. So, if Rory held no interest in Sheffield's papers, then they weren't all that stimulating to begin with. Besides, she had her own research she needed to focus on. And one of her subjects sat before her, giving her his undivided attention. It would be best if she put her valuable time to use.

"So, if we cannot discuss Sheffield's papers due to my lack of not finding them, let us discuss the man himself. What is your opinion of Sheffield's character?" Sidney inquired.

"Well if that is not a loaded question, I don't know what is," laughed Rory.

"How so?"

"You wish for me to give my judgment on the very gentleman who courts you."

"What is wrong with that? I value your opinion and would like to know what you think of him."

"If you are inquiring if I think he is husband material for you, the answer to that is no. But then again, I am biased toward you and would say the same for any competition for your hand."

"Competition?"

"Yes, Sidney. You are being competed for, if by any indication of your mother's crowded parlor yesterday. I have decided to throw my hat in as well."

"You wish to court me?" Sidney asked, dumbfounded.

Rory stood and walked around the desk, tugging Sidney out of her chair and into his arms. While it felt natural to hold her in his arms, it did not feel complete. It was a new experience for them and would take time. Their bond of friendship now turned into a courtship. It was an odd experience for them, but one that felt content. He tipped her chin up to meet his eyes. As he stared into them, he noted her confusion, and something else he couldn't quite figure out. It was if her mind tried to process information and separate it into compartments. This wasn't how he wanted this scene to play. He needed to shock her in order to place himself at the forefront of her mind.

What Rory didn't realize was that was exactly what Sidney did. Her plans to draw the interest of her three chosen gentlemen fell in the palm of her hands today. This latest development with Rory was more than she expected. He shocked her when he pulled her into his arms, but it felt nice and content. What more could a girl ask for? She was unprepared for what he tried next. After he tipped her head, he lowered his head in an attempt to kiss her. She must stop him. This moved way too fast. Luckily, her father's footsteps in the hall and his request of tea and cookies saved her. Rory swiftly drew his arms away from her and moved over to the shelves, pulling out a book. Sidney rested her hand on her cheek against the warm blush that covered her face. At the sound of her father's footsteps drew nearer, she moved to open the window. The fresh air perfumed the study and cooled her in one shot.

"Ah, perfect, you two are already here. I need both of your help and opinions on the matter of the discovery of Lord Hemingsworth's find. He swears it's an ancient relic from the twelfth century, but I'm beginning to believe his gardener presented this artifact to his lordship to save his job. Now where did I lay that paperwork?" Sidney's father mumbled as he came into his study.

"I believe your notes are right here, Papa," Sidney replied, risking a glance at Rory.

Rory watched in amusement as a flustered Sidney cooled her reaction to him and tried to appear calm before her father. When she looked his way, he sent her an innocent smile of charm. She frowned at him as she located her father's papers. Lord Hartridge was unaware of the newly developed tension between the two, oblivious to his daughter's emotions, which was for the best. Rory didn't want to explain his actions to Lord Hartridge, or to his daughter for that matter. No, it was definitely better to keep Sidney wondering on the new development of his attraction toward her. It would draw her interest more than anything. He settled back in the chair he previously occupied as Lord Hartridge explained his findings.

Emerson soon interrupted them with the afternoon tea and a message for Sidney that Sophia waited for her in the garden. Lord Hartridge waved her away, promising her he would inform her of his discovery later. Before she could leave the study, she had to pass by Rory's chair. She avoided eye contact with him. Not wanting to leave her thoughts, he brushed his hand across her fingers as she moved past him. He heard her gasp, and he smiled as she rushed out of the room. Yes, Sidney Hartridge would not forget him so easily today.

Chapter Six

Sidney hurried to the garden to meet Phee. Not wanting to keep her friend waiting, she picked up her pace into a run, only to stop short as she came along the path where her friend sat on a bench talking to a gentleman. Not any gentleman, but the one never far from her thoughts since she first met him. Noah Wildeburg held a deep conversation with Phee, with his head bent toward her to capture her every word. The intimate discussion confused Sidney. And sparked her jealousy, which was nonsense. She was not jealous of her friend. If Phee could find happiness with somebody of Wildeburg's reputation, then she wished them the best. Only, she felt a strong connection to Wildeburg on many levels herself.

She backed around the corner, pasted a smile on her face, and called out a greeting to her friend. As she came back around the corner again, it was to find Wildeburg on his feet at a respectable distance from Phee. Sophia rested on the bench with a secretive smile gracing her face as she gazed adoringly at Lord Wildeburg. Sidney felt like an interloper on a budding relationship.

"Lord Wildeburg, what a surprise. Emerson did not make me aware of your visit."

"I'm afraid I am intruding. I came upon Lady Sophia sitting all alone as I walked by and decided to keep her company."

"It is highly improper of you, My Lord. You should have called at the front door," Sidney reprimanded him.

"My apologies, Lady Sidney. Thank you for our delightful conversation, Lady Sophia. I bid you ladies a wonderful afternoon." Wildeburg bowed before he left the garden.

"Sid, your behavior was rude. Lord Wildeburg acted as a complete gentleman."

Sidney grimaced at her own rudeness. Her jealousy overtook her emotions, and she understood how badly she behaved toward him. She slumped next to Phee and rested her head on her shoulder.

"I'm sorry, Phee. Please forgive my rudeness. I am so confused."

"Your apology needs to be directed to Lord Wildeburg. Also, I believe he hoped to catch you in the garden, not I."

"I am not so sure of that. You two appeared pretty friendly with your heads together."

"Yes, well ..." Phee drifted off.

Sidney lifted her head to notice Phee had a dreamy expression on her face. She wanted to know what they discussed but held herself back from asking. Whatever they chatted about must have been a private conversation between the two. She needed to put her own attraction to Wildeburg to the side now—for her friend's happiness. Besides, attraction was only a fleeting emotion, the kind that never lasted. While lust disappeared as fast as it appeared, it was love Sidney desired the most. Love would endure the test of time. If Sophia felt love for Wildeburg, then Sidney must make sure his intentions were true. All the more reason to discover what his actions were.

"What are you confused about, Sidney?" Phee interrupted Sidney's thoughts.

"My three subjects, what else?"

"Tell me about your interactions, and I will help you process your confusion."

"Who do I start with?" Sid sighed.

"Well let us start with the least of your troubles, Rory."

"He is not the least of my troubles. He is ranking right up there with my other subjects." Sidney rose from the bench and paced across the garden path.

"How so?"

"Right before I came outside, we shared a couple of moments in the study."

"Please sit, Sidney. You are making me dizzy with your pacing."

"I can't, you know this is how I process information. I need to sort out my feelings so I can understand how to continue with my study."

"All right, but at least slow down. What has Rory done that has you so rattled?"

"Well, for starters, he declared his intentions to court me, then he pulled me in his arms and was about to kiss me before we heard Papa in the hallway. Then as I passed him on my way out of the study, he brushed his fingers across mine in an intimate gesture." Sidney ticked off Rory's actions on her fingers as she listed them out for Phee.

Sophia stared at Sidney in shock. Rory's actions surprised her. Ever since Rory entered their lives as a friend, he only ever portrayed a brotherly connection to both women. He was good-natured and protected them from scoundrels, always good for a laugh or a thoughtful conversation. Never once did he display an attraction toward them. Sure, he was a handsome fellow, and any lady would be lucky to have him, but their friendship with him never pointed in that direction until now. Sophia feared her friend got herself in over her head. This was only one of her subjects. Phee was eager to hear what else Sidney experienced. If the behavior of their close friend was any indication, Sid was doomed.

"Close your mouth, Phee, before you eat a bug."

"Well, I must admit, your encounter with Rory is shocking. Before I even try to understand his actions, fill me in with your visits with the other two men. I understand Sheffield took you for a ride this morning, and I'm only guessing you had a visit from Wildeburg too. Am I correct on this?"

"Two visits."

"With Sheffield?"

"No, Wildeburg."

"Wildeburg? Now I am dying to learn more. First tell me about Sheffield. I'm sure he was dull as dirt. That is, if you could get past his arrogant, pompous attitude. Yes, leave the delicious Wildeburg for the end. How was your ride with Sheffield?"

"Sophia Turlington, that is a vulgar opinion of Sheffield, even for you."

"Yes, but it is nothing that is not true. I am only calling it like I see it."

"Phee, you never talk negative about a single soul. Why such a strong reaction to Sheffield?"

"Something he declared regarding you."

"And that was?"

"Nevermind, I do not want it to influence your research. You must keep an unbiased opinion on your subjects and not be manipulated by outside sources."

"Phee …"

"No, Rory made me to realize Sheffield's words are not worth getting upset over. He explained that you will see through any smoke and mirrors to understand a person's true character."

"Rory declared all that?"

"No, but it is the conclusion I drew from his reaction. I won't tell you either, Sid, until you finish your research. So, you will not attempt this discussion again. Also, you will not ask Rory, because he will tell you whatever you want to hear to further his chances for your hand."

Sidney growled her frustration. "All right, you are correct as usual."

"So, onto Sheffield. How was your outing in the park?"

Sidney finally settled on the bench, drawing her legs up to rest her chin on her knees as she described her adventure this morning. She then told Phee how Sheffield pulled the curricle into a secluded spot and explained their interaction in full detail. Every action from his touch, to her touch, and everything that happened after that. If Sidney stunned Phee earlier with Rory's new attitude, it was nothing compared to how she felt about Sheffield's reaction. Phee's mouth once again hung open in surprise, only this time her eyes grew larger too. Her friend's reaction would have been comical if Sidney wasn't so confused herself. Sid went on to explain how Wildeburg interrupted them before Sheffield kissed her. She then continued to share with Phee the entire exchange, concluding with her conversation with Sheffield on the front stoop.

"Sidney you almost achieved today alone, the results for your experiment with Rory and Sheffield."

"I am aware of that, Sophia. The gentlemen of the aristocracy are all scoundrels, our friend included. This whole thing is moving faster than I ever imagined. I thought it would require months to collect the data that has taken me less than a week to accumulate."

"And Wildeburg? Has he given you any data to compare with Sheffield and Rory?"

Phee watched her friend blush at the mention of Lord Wildeburg's name. Sophia felt Sidney held an attraction to the gentleman. She watched as they danced at the Woodsworths' ball. Phee observed the connection simmering between the two when they interacted, and it seemed that both of them were oblivious. It would also appear that Sidney had spent time alone with the wild marquess. From her recent conversation with Lord Wildeburg, he was smitten with Sidney and wished for her help to further his cause. While Phee questioned his full intention, she could tell he had fallen under Sidney's charm. His charming attitude settled Phee into an ease that before long she disclosed with him Sidney's likes and dislikes in full detail. He appeared genuinely interested in Sidney.

Phee understood Sidney's desire to expose the rascals of the ton, but she also felt her friend deserved a happily ever after. Of all the men Sidney collected data on, Wildeburg seemed the perfect match for her friend. So, while Sidney did her experiment, Phee decided she would do her own. Her experiment was to find her friend a match for the season, and Lord Wildeburg suited Sid to a tee. Besides being an absolute charmer, he was very sexy. There was enough chemistry between the two for an explosion, one Phee would be more than happy to ignite. Sheffield was a boor and didn't deserve Sidney. Rory might be a friend, but his mixed emotions only confused the situation. Phee would have to make Rory understand, in a polite manner, how absurd his intentions were. As for Sheffield, she would endure putting herself in between him and Sidney for her friend to have a chance at love.

"Only the dance we shared and our time with Sheffield earlier." Sidney lied again to Phee. She didn't want to discuss their time alone in the park. It was a private moment she was not yet ready to share.

"What conclusions do you draw from your interactions?"

"He is definitely a charmer. His comments about a wife and her duties astounded me. He displayed actions I would not have thought a rogue would. His behavior is one of a hero in those romance novels you read, charming and caring to his devoted love. I know it sounds weird. We all know no gentleman would behave that way and mean it."

"Why is that so hard to believe?"

"Phee, you don't believe in the rubbish you read?"

"Yes, as a matter of fact, I do. I believe any man with the right lady would treat his beloved the way those stories convey. If you would let your softer side emerge outside of your intellectual side, you would envision the same outcome."

"I value our friendship too much to dissuade you from your own beliefs. If this is how you imagine true love, then I wish you all the luck in discovering this passion."

Sophia sighed as she reached for Sidney's hand. "My friend, one day this passion will consume you, and then you shall see I am correct. I only hope you embrace the moment and simply enjoy."

"Mmm," was the only reply Sidney offered Sophia.

"So now, how will you proceed?"

"At the Havelock Ball, I will attempt to draw each gentleman into the garden to sample a kiss."

"I thought you only wanted to see if they tried to get you alone to kiss you. Now you want them to actually kiss you?"

"I must. Each man has affected me differently. I need to understand why I am attracted to each of them."

"Sidney, that is going too far. You run too much of a chance of getting caught. Then your parents will force you into a marriage with one you do not desire."

"That is where I will require your help. You will follow me to the garden with each gentleman and send me a warning if we are about to be caught. Also, you will interrupt us if they attempt liberties beyond a simple kiss."

"I still think this is a horrible idea."

"Maybe, but it is one for the greater good. You must remember our friends who were ruined; this will give me the final data for my research. Then I can write a paper and expose the scoundrels of the ton and their ruses to lure innocent misses to ruination. Sophia, consider how this information will aid every new debutante."

"I suppose so. Will you promise me one thing? If one of your subjects happen to be your soul mate, you will end this experiment and open your heart to love."

"I promise, not that there stands a chance for any such nonsense."

Sophia bid her farewell to Sidney, leaving her alone in the garden. Love? She shook her head at the silly notion. Her friend spent too much time reading about romance. Phee considered every gentleman's attention a gesture toward a relationship, while most of the time they only displayed kindness. Sophia was naïve when it came to the character traits of men. True, Sidney secretly read those same stories, but she was more realistic with a man's true nature. During the time she worked with her father and involved herself in his discussions, she recognized men for who they really were. They were domineering, conceited, and only looked at topics with a one-sided opinion. There were a few rare exceptions: her father for one and Rory a close second. Perhaps Rory was an ideal mate. He always protected and valued her opinions without trying to change her mind. Even though he didn't make her heart go pitter-patter, he was a fine-looking fellow. What more could a girl ask for?

She could ask for a fellow who made her feel soft inside and gave her a dreamy expression when she thought of him. One whose touch made her shiver for more. One who had thick blond hair, she wished to run her fingers through, while his bedroom eyes devoured her. One who she wished would kiss her. One who stood before her?

Sidney shook her head to clear her thoughts, closing her eyes. Now she was imagining him in her garden. This wasn't a good sign for her sanity. As she heard a throat clear, she opened her eyes. To see standing before her, the man who invaded her thoughts.

"Excuse me for interrupting you again, but I wanted to apologize for my earlier behavior."

"You want to apologize for the very behavior you are repeating again?"

Wildeburg smiled at her quick wit. "I was hoping this token would excuse my actions," he replied as he held out his hands to her.

In his hands he held a small package of her favorite butterscotch candy, wrapped in Sampson's paper and tied with a red bow. A piece of candy was hanging from the ribbon. Sampson made the best candy in Piccadilly. He moved his hand closer for her to take the sweets. When she hesitated, he undid the ribbon and pulled out a piece for himself. After no movement from her, he undid the wrapper and popped the butterscotch into his mouth. He closed his eyes and released a moan of delight as he savored the candy. Sidney's mouth watered at the treat he enjoyed. She also gulped as she gazed at him enjoying the candy. His pleasure seemed almost sensual. Sidney's teeth scraped her upper lip, biting down as she watched him. As he licked his lips, Sidney's reaction was to lick hers too.

When Wilde opened his eyes, he thought he would find a disgruntled lady, agitated at him for invading her private sanctuary. Instead, his eyes encountered midnight eyes growing dark with desire. As he stared, her tongue slid over her lips, as if she herself savored the sweet candy. Her lips glistened as they begged for him to kiss her, to have her sample the butterscotch from his mouth. He took a step toward her, startling her out of her daydream. When her eyes met with his, he noticed her confusion. He kept forgetting she was an inexperienced miss. While he was aware of the full impact of their attraction, she was not. There was nothing he wanted to do more than to draw her into his embrace and show her the passion they could share. But he understood that would scare her away. He would frighten her into somebody's else's arms. Sheffield's arms. No, he would need to slow down his chase. Slow and steady wins the race.

Wilde cleared his throat. "As I was saying, an apology." He placed the candy on her lap and bowed before her. With a smile, he took his leave and left the garden as quietly as he entered, never giving her a chance to comment.

Sidney continued to sit on the bench in confusion. What just happened? She was unable to come to a conclusion over her muddled thoughts. Her emotions in the last few moments changed from caution, to desire, to bewilderment, to an utter state of awe. How could one man hold such an impact on her emotions? She wanted to explore her attraction to Wildeburg, but to do that, she ran the risk of a broken heart. Sidney had an inclination it would be worth it. To experience what he offered her would be a once in a lifetime chance. Why wouldn't she want to grab it?

As she glanced to her lap, she took notice of his sweet gesture. Sidney smiled as she unwrapped a piece and popped the candy into her mouth. She moaned. It was delicious. No wonder Wildeburg moaned his delight at the flavor. As she replayed the scene in her mind, not once did she stop to question how he knew the flavor of her favorite candy.

~~~~~~

Wildeburg sauntered into White's with the swagger of a man satisfied with himself. He sent nods to acquaintances and cocky grins to those who disapproved of his actions. As he settled into the cushioned leather seat in Sheffield's private room of the club, he waited for his friend to acknowledge him. When he continued to be ignored, his smile only grew more confident. For when Sheffield ignored someone, he was irritated with them. This only meant he held more of a chance with Sidney Hartridge than Alex did. Yes, another score for him.

Sheffield was well aware Wildeburg sat across from him with a smug grin on his face. He watched as he strutted into the club, sure of himself. Before he caught his eye, Sheffield pulled the newspaper in front of his face and pretended to read. He was beyond irritated with the fool. This morning in the park, Wilde stated his intentions with Sidney Hartridge loud and clear. Wilde meant to pursue her and to give Sheffield a run for his money. He couldn't let him know how much it bothered him. If Wilde sniffed the scent of competition, then it would become a contest of who was the most superior man. Sidney Hartridge didn't deserve to be played as a game. While the lady used to annoy him, he grew to respect her after the last couple of days spent in her company. She took stock of a situation and analyzed it before she responded. She was no simple-minded miss, and for that, he owed her the respect she deserved.

His conversation with her father earlier only confirmed his decision to not tempt Wilde into a contest. Sheffield had warned Lord Hartridge of Wildeburg, but her father only brushed the warning aside, muttering that Sidney was a grown woman and could look after herself. He even informed Sheffield that Sidney was the only one to offer permission on his suit. He wouldn't be the one marrying him, so it would be pointless to agree to scare away any other gentlemen who might wish to court her. The earl was as unpredictable with his daughter as he was with his research. Any other father of the ton who realized a duke courted their daughter would decline all invites from any other gentlemen. But not Lord Hartridge, he encouraged the more the merrier. As a sign of respect to their family, he would take it upon himself to remove any threat. The other chaps would be easy to discourage, but Wildeburg would be harder to shake.

He saw the attraction between the two, even though Lady Sidney displayed no behavior to the contrary. Her innocence made her unaware of the sizzling atmosphere. He needed to make sure Wilde didn't expose her to the emotion. To have Noah discontinue his pursuit of Lady Sidney Hartridge, he must pretend his own indifference to the lady. When Wilde realized there would be no contest, he would grow tired of the innocent miss and find other delights within his grasp. Perhaps if he were to show interest in another lady, Wilde would move on from the trick he was playing.

"How long are you going to continue to ignore me, old chap?"

"As long as it takes for you to accept the hint and leave."

Wilde released a bellow of laughter. "Never."

Sheffield sighed and lowered the newspaper, folded it, and placed it next to his drink on the table in front of him. As he grabbed his drink, he leaned back in the chair and swirled the liquid around in his glass before he took a sip.

"Not your usual scene this late at night. I'm sure Belle is missing you."

"More you than me. She was disappointed to hear you would not be visiting her anymore."

"Yes, well her establishment is not a location where I can be seen during this time."

"You misunderstand. Her sadness is not from missing your coin, but your company instead."

"A friendship I cannot continue during my search for a bride. Perhaps later."

"After you're married then?"

"Of course. When else? Belle will understand. I shall send her a message on my predicament. She is a woman who is aware of the restrictions of my status as a duke."

"So, after your wedding, you plan to continue where you left off."

"After a considerable amount of time, I see no reason my life should alter just because I've taken a bride."

"You would embarrass a lady as special as Sidney Hartridge with mistresses?"

"A common occurrence of the ton. You of all men understand that. Or are the married women you trifle with innocent in their actions?"

Wilde sat in silence at Alex's words. Harsh as they might have been, they held truth in their unspoken depths. As grand of a prize as Lady Sidney was, why would Sheffield abuse what could be a promising marriage? If a husband and a wife shared a deep connection, why would a husband stray? Or a wife for that matter? Why not nurture said relationship as it developed into a love everlasting? Wilde paused in his thoughts. Where did that drivel come from? He laughed to himself. It must have come from the damn novel he read. The absurd book almost made him believe in the promise of one mate and a happily ever after. How ironic for him to imagine that scene. Sheffield was correct. It was only natural he would stray, as well as any gentleman of the aristocracy. It was their culture; any lady would assume their husband kept a mistress on the side.

"Whether it be Lady Sidney or any other lady I will court this season, the outcome will be the same. I will devote my time to her until she is with child. Then I shall resume my pleasures," Sheffield explained.

While he became lost in his thoughts of romance, Sheffield declared something about other girls he would chase this season. Did he hear correct that Lady Sidney wasn't his only option? If so, his own hunt for her hand was for naught. While they held a connection he didn't understand, he only chased her to prove to Sheffield that no woman would choose anybody over himself.

"Lady Sidney is not your only candidate?"

Sheffield laughed. "Not by far. She happened to be the first. There are many ladies who hold my interest to court. A man cannot settle for mediocre when he can have the grandest being offered."

"You find her lacking then?"

"Mmm, let us say she possesses a few faults I don't know if I can overlook."

"You seemed to overlook a few of her faults at the park this morning. From what I witnessed, you appeared close to sampling a few of her charms."

"Yes, as I was saying, I need to know if the lady I choose to become my bride meets all my requirements. Plus, she directed a few of her own signals my way. I only acted on what she offered."

Wilde stood and advanced toward Sheffield. His eyes narrowed as his lips tightened in anger at the insult. He leaned over his friend to drag him from his chair and place a planter on his face. When he encountered Sheffield's haughty smirk, he realized he might have spoken the truth. It was not like him to defend a lady's honor. Also, it would appear Alex played his own game with him. To find out the truth, Wilde retreated to his chair.

"What signals would those be?"

"A true gentleman does not kiss and tell."

"So, you two shared a kiss? I thought I interrupted you before you had the chance."

"Yes, well it was not as if you were present during our entire outing, were you?"

Sheffield had him there, but he knew when his friend lied, which he mostly definitely was. Wilde took notice of every ounce of her while in their company, and she wasn't a lady who had been recently kissed. Her lips were untouched. If Sheffield kissed her, he didn't kiss her the way she deserved. Her lips were not full, red, or pouted from being savored. No, Sheffield played him for a fool. He would appear to fall for his lies while he observed his actions.

"Who are your other choices?"

"Why are you so interested? Do you plan to chase their skirts too?"

"Afraid of the competition, mate?"

"No. By all means, compete."

Wilde stood as he realized their conversation gained him no results. Sheffield was a fool not to think Lady Sidney was the perfect mate. If his friend were to court other ladies, then he would warn Lady Sidney and at least protect her from any hurt she might suffer at the hands of Sheffield.

Then he would chase the other ladies to make sure Alex got what he deserved in his search for a perfect mate.

"Give Belle my love."

Wilde raised his hand as he acknowledged Sheffield's sly remark. Let him believe he still frequented Belle's establishment. What could it hurt? As he paused outside the club, he waved away an offer for a ride with a group of young gentlemen who left the club. They were on their way to a card game, and he declined their offer, to their groans of disappointment. While any other night he would have led the charge to one indiscretion after another, tonight his heart was not in it. He walked for a spell, his thoughts leading his steps to an unknown destination. Before long, he stopped and leaned against the street post, the glow of the lantern lost in the fog, keeping him in the shadows. He stood outside the home of the lady who consumed his thoughts.

Chapter Seven

Darkness cloaked the Hartridges' townhome. When he left his club, the clock had chimed ten o'clock. They either retired to bed early, or he had walked longer than he thought. Wilde wondered which bedroom hers was. He imagined her to have a room that faced the garden, where she could admire the beautiful flowers as they bloomed. He moved quietly toward the fence on the side of their townhome. When he opened the gate, he waited for a screech that never came. Wilde smiled at his luck as he continued to the back of the house. As he stood in the middle of the garden, he noticed the soft light appearing in the window next to the trellis. It had to be her room. Should he? Why not? Was that not what he was known for?

Wilde shook off his coat and suit jacket, laying them across the bench he sat on earlier in the day. The same spot where he tempted her to eat the sweet candy. Where he gazed as her eyes turned dark with desire. He rattled the trellis to judge the sturdiness of his climbing apparatus. Satisfied it was secured to the house, he began his climb. When he reached her window, he peered in through the curtain to find her at her desk. The cool night air blew through the slightly cracked window.

Her head was bent as she swiftly wrote across a piece of paper. She reached the bottom of the page, where she flipped the parchment over and started on another. Her pen dipped into the ink as she continued on. Wilde's curiosity drew him to know what captivated her attention so thoroughly. She was a mystery he wanted to solve. A smile spread across his face as she slid the butterscotch candy between her lips. With every dip of her pen into the ink, she treated herself to a bite of candy. Each morsel she savored, she closed her eyes for a brief second in pleasure. Suddenly, she set down her pen and lifted the sheets of vellum to read her work. As she glanced over her notes, she licked the candy off her fingers. When she slid her finger in her mouth and slowly sucked on her fingers, Wilde moved his body forward, entranced with the sight, and lost his foothold on the lattice. His foot slipped on the wet rung, and his body scrambled to hold on. To make matters worse, the gentle rain turned into a downpour, which caused him to loosen his grip. He realized if he didn't reach the window ledge, he would fall off the trellis and land in a painful mess in the garden. With such a racket, he would surely awaken Lord Hartridge and create a scandal for their family. A scandal that would earn him a bride he didn't wish for at this moment. Then why did he climb a trellis and attempt to climb into her room? It was a question he could not answer, nor did he want to.

Wilde regained his hold on the trellis, with one arm he reached for the window ledge and swung his body onto the wide landing. After he recovered his balance, he lowered his body and lifted the window higher. He slid inside and landed in a heap on her carpeted floor. It was a soft landing for him, and dry too. He closed his eyes and sighed at his relief to be inside, instead of outside in the pouring rain.

Sidney gasped as her window rose and the wind blew the curtains off the ground. She was even more surprised when a man rolled through the window and fell onto her floor. She pushed her chair back and rushed over to stand above the intruder. Sidney held the fire poker above her head, ready to attack. As she gazed at the man lying on her floor, her surprise soon turned to disbelief. Noah Wildeburg lay on her floor with his arms spread wide and a look of contentment upon his face. She lowered the fire poker, propped it against her bed, and lowered her fist onto her hips. She glared at him as she waited for him to open his eyes.

Wilde knew she stood above him, probably in a huff for his intrusion on her domain. His grin grew as he imagined her in a fury. He slit his eyes open, just wide enough to view her, but his gaze became distracted by the sheer white nightgown illuminated by the fire behind her. His smile disappeared, replaced by an inner moan. She was stunning as her long legs and high breasts graced his eyes. He desired to take in her full beauty but knew she would cover herself when she became aware of the direction of his vision. But his fingers had a mind of their own. Before he realized his actions, his hand reached to touch the softness of her skin. Wilde wrapped his hand around her ankle and slid his palm along her leg. He released a moan at the silkiness of her body.

Sidney's eyes grew wide at his bold touch. The flurry of sensations enveloping her body sent her thoughts into a mere blur. Her mind became incoherent as her leg tingled with the path his fingers journeyed. His moan invaded her senses, and her common sense took hold. She lifted the poker and tried to whack at his head to attract his notice. Only the curtain blew out and knocked her off balance. She dropped the poker, missing him by inches. Sidney became tangled in his arms.

His arms tightened around her as he drew her flush to his body. When her hands rested on his chest, his warmth seared the wet garment. She raised her head to meet his eyes, which held the same confusion she felt. Sidney's heartbeat quickened as the confusion disappeared into desire. Wilde's head lifted off the floor as her head bent toward him, both of their bodies on their own accord but one with each other.

Their lips met, slowly brushing across to meet again for more of a taste, each kiss gentle to the touch. His mouth opened as his tongue slid to coax her mouth open wider. As she obliged, he explored the sweetness of Sidney Hartridge. Wilde savored the candy she devoured and moaned into her mouth. When she responded to him, he became hungry for more. His kisses turned more passionate, showing her his desire. Soon she responded to the same level of his passion. It wasn't enough, he wanted to sample more. He pulled her tighter to him as his kisses became a hunger only she could sate. His hands roamed over her sheer nightgown as he tugged it up her body, wanting to touch her silken skin. Wilde's touch turned bolder than he intended.

His lips drew her to him, and she became hypnotized by the desire in his eyes. Her inexperience with kissing went unnoticed to Wildeburg as he guided her along on the passion he inflamed. When his caresses changed to something more powerful than she ever imagined or read about, she floated lost in his spell. Each nip and stroke of his tongue created a powerful draw to him, one she no longer wished to deny herself. Soon she felt his hands stroke her body, and she softened against him, moaning into their kisses.

A gust of wind and rain blew into the bedroom and awakened Sidney to her ruination. Rain pelted against the bare legs he uncovered. Sidney pulled away, and her knee dug into his stomach as she struggled out of his arms. Her own behavior stunned her. Wildeburg rolled around on the floor in agony as he grabbed at his stomach. Sidney took full notice of the marquess and how his wet clothes clung to him. He was a man who took care of himself, despite his late-night carousing. Muscles gripped his arms, and his stomach was flat. Sidney's eyes wandered lower over his muscled thighs and lingered near one area. She wasn't naïve about a man's anatomy. The research she performed with her father educated her in this area. Wildeburg's desire strained against the placket of his trousers. Even in pain, he still held an arousal. Sidney bit her bottom lip as she continued to admire him.

Wilde should not be so aroused with the pain in his stomach. Nonetheless, he was. Any man would be if they stared at Sidney Hartridge before them in a wet nightdress, as she centered her eyesight on their cock. When her teeth tugged at her bottom lip and she continued to stare, he only grew harder. What made it worse was that she had no clue how her reaction affected him. A complete innocent. Who be it for him to not allow a lady a glance? If she were to stare, then so would he until she realized she stood before him in a wet nightgown.

The wet garment showed him more than before, every curve outlined to detail. Her breasts were full, and her nipples were pressed tight against the fabric. Their rosy tips begged for him to rise and take them between his lips. Wilde shut his eyes as he groaned loudly at the image before him.

His groan was loud enough to wake her parents if they were not such sound sleepers, stopped her bold examination. She stepped over his body when she moved to shut the window. As she turned toward him to reprimand his rude behavior, she discovered his eyes fastened on her nightgown. When she bent her head, she realized why. With her gown plastered to her body, she displayed herself to him as if she were naked. She rushed to the screen and yanked on her dressing gown. Sidney stormed back to him and held out her hand as she pointed at the window.

"Out. Get out. Right this instance. Have you no shame?"

Wilde laughed as he came to his feet; shame was his middle name. He ignored her anger and roamed around her room. He picked up her knickknacks and then set them back down again. As he approached her desk, she swiftly followed him, scooped up her papers, and slid them into a drawer. Obviously, they were not something she wanted anybody to read. He fingered the ribbon wrapped around the candy and turned to her.

"I notice you are enjoying my treat."

"Nonsense. I gave them to my maid."

"Mmm, I could have sworn I tasted them on your lips. Lips that are most delicious tasting all on their own."

"Leave this instance before I scream. You, sir, are a scoundrel of the highest order."

"And you, my dear, are a piece of candy I am newly addicted to."

"Do you not realize the consequences of your actions? I will not be forced to wed you."

Wilde reached to touch a curl, clinging to her neck. "No act between us will be performed under force, my sweet," he whispered.

Sidney stood still at his words. Once again, she drowned in the essence of Wildeburg. His touch and voice lured her to him. She took a hesitant step toward him, then stopped as she tried to pull away from the attraction. He lowered his hand and walked to the window. When he raised the glass to leave, she stopped him.

"Why?"

He turned around and shrugged his shoulders. "An impulse," he answered.

He slipped out the window and climbed down the trellis. Sidney rushed to the opening and stared as he landed in the garden. Once he landed, Wildeburg strolled over to the bench to slide on his jacket and coat. When he turned around, he blew her a kiss. Sidney heard the soft whistle of a song as he sauntered from the garden.

"An impulse?" she murmured as she touched her fingers to her lips.

~~~~~

Sidney wiped the water off the bench with her handkerchief. The rain from the evening before created a drenched atmosphere in the park. She opened the paper sack she carried and tossed out the bread crumbs. Before long, the ducks waddled toward her for the special treat. A grin graced her face as two ducks fought over the food. When the bigger duck devoured the bread, the smaller duck wandered away. Taking pity on the small creature, she rose and headed toward the duck. When she approached the animal, she lowered herself to talk quietly, while offering the smaller duck the remainder of her bag. Sidney laughed as the small animal nibbled on the rest of her bread. Her laughter brought on the attention of the other ducks, who soon swarmed her, as they wanted more too. When a couple of ducks attacked her, she released a scream and swatted her arms to keep them at bay.

Soon an arm swept her aside as an umbrella poked at the ducks. "Get, get."

Once the ducks scattered back to the pond, Sidney glanced at her rescuer. It was none other than Lord Wildeburg, the same gentleman who caused her a restless night sleep. Her emotions were on edge when she awoke, and she headed to the park to gather her thoughts. He was as handsome wearing an overcoat, dry as can be, as he was compared to the evening before when he was drenched wet in her bedchamber. The wind ruffled his hair at the ends, and the overcast sky didn't impact the charming smile he bestowed upon her. Sidney felt frumpy next to him. She donned an old dress for her hasty excursion, and her hair was piled atop her head haphazardly, with stray strands tousled along her neck. Sidney didn't think she would see anybody this morning. It was early yet, with not a soul in sight, except for him.

"Did you come to any harm?"

"No, My Lord, but then I was never in harm's way."

Wilde laughed at her denial. She was a delight. Her refusal to admit to his aid only endured her to him more. As he took in her appearance, he noted the subtle changes to her clothes. She appeared before him comfortable and at home in her simple dress. Also, he found the thrown-together hairstyle attractive on her. She held the appearance of a lady who had just risen from bed. Her blue eyes held a sleepy look, likely from the result of a sleepless night. Did she dream of him? Lord knows he dreamed of her. He had lain in bed for countless hours thinking of their kiss. He finally rose after sleep eluded him. With Lady Sidney on his mind, he decided to visit the park near her home. His wishful thoughts led him to hope she would also be here. As luck would have it, she was.

"No, of course you weren't."

Sidney had no reply. She realized her attitude was defensive but could not help herself. She knew of no other way to handle her emotions around him. Sidney stared as he scrutinized her appearance. Instead of holding disgust with her form, his eyes took on the same dreamy gaze from the previous night when he kissed her. Sidney raised her hand and patted at her head as she tried to control her hair. It was useless. The strands loosened, and her hair tangled around her face.

They stood facing each other while neither one of them said a word. Both of their breaths caught as her hair blew behind her. His because her hair was loose and flowing and hers because of the look his eyes held. His dreamy gaze soon turned into a heavy stare filled with a need that consumed her. She needed to speak, to break the moment, but could find no words to complete the action.

Wilde took a step toward her, but when her eyes met his and confusion clouded her vision, he stopped himself. He pulled his hands behind his back to keep them from drawing her into his arms. He realized after his intrusion into her bedroom that he needed to court her properly. And if he enclosed her into his embrace while he ravished her mouth in the open park, it would not earn him a spot on her dance card.

"Are you following me?"

"In a slight way, I suppose I am."

"Slight way?"

"Not deliberate, but hopeful."

"Hopeful? You, My Lord, make no sense. Are you following me or not?"

"No, I did not follow you from your home. But I walked to the park, hoping you would be here. So, you could say my wishful thoughts drew my steps down the same path as yours."

"Is this part of your famous charm that you use to draw the ladies into your web?"

"Is it working?" he asked as he waggled his eyebrows.

Sidney couldn't help herself and giggled. She had to hand it to him, his charm oozed from him so naturally. She now understood why the fallen maidens and widows held a fascination with him. His way with words confused them, yet captivated them enough to want to listen to more. Sidney fell hard for his charm.

"I will never tell. A secret I shall keep close to my heart," she flirted back.

"A secret I must discover."

Sidney smiled over her shoulder at him as she wandered to the bench. She sat and stared at the pond, watching the ducks swim. She knew he would follow her, and she was not mistaken. He slid next to her, closer than properly allowed. His warmth enveloped her as he blocked the cool wind. When his hand drew her hair back, she didn't stop him. She shouldn't allow his touch, but she craved more. His fingers slid under her chin and turned her face toward his. She should pull away and leave the park now. As she stayed close to him, she allowed him to tease her into ruination, which was foolish on her part. But her curiosity had always been her downfall.

When she didn't draw away, he slid his hand to cup her cheek and lowered his lips to hers. He softly brushed across them once, then twice. When she still didn't resist, he coaxed her mouth open under his. He kissed her gently as he drew out each kiss slowly. Wilde savored the taste of her lips with his. When he heard her moan, he deepened the kiss.

The sudden noise of a horse galloping along the path tore him out of her arms as he stood a respectable distance from her. The horse had yet to reach the clearing when he addressed her.

"I will not apologize for my kiss, even though I should. I must leave before we are spotted together. Please inform me where I may find you this evening."

Confused by the loss of his lips and the intrusion that would soon be upon them, she answered him before she realized she shouldn't. "The Steadhampton Musical."

"I promise I will see you then." Wildeburg departed in the woods near the pond.

Once again, he disappeared while he spoke the last word. Sidney held her fingers to her lips as she sat in awe of the gentle kiss he bestowed upon her. The caress was quite different from the previous night. Last night's kiss promised a passionate desire, this one a gentle affection, as if he held as much doubt as she did if they should kiss. Today's kiss wrapped her in a sense of security. An emotion Wildeburg would not usually evoke on a lady.

Suddenly, the horse they had heard a few moments ago stopped. When she turned around, Sheffield lowered himself to the ground and rushed to her side. His groom followed behind them and controlled the horses.

"There you are. I stopped by your home to see if you wanted to ride, but your mother told me I could find you here."

"What a lovely idea, but I'm afraid mother nature has a different idea," Sidney replied as raindrops fell upon their heads.

"Well in that case, perhaps we should seek shelter instead."

He glanced around for a location to hide from the storm. When he spotted the gazebo nearby, he guided her under the small roof. As they gazed at the rain, he noticed her body shiver. Sheffield shrugged off his overcoat and rested it upon her shoulders. She smiled her gratitude to him and murmured a small thank you. When she turned back to the rain, he realized her gaze strayed to a group of trees near the pond. He wondered why, but as his eyes adjusted through the wet air, he understood why. Wildeburg. His friend had once again beaten him at the game they played. He realized the rascal still waited in the trees when a movement confirmed his suspicions.

When he looked more closely at Lady Sidney, he noticed her hair fell around her shoulders, and her lips were full and pouty from being kissed. The devil wasted no time. He'd already moved onto the seduction. Well two could play at that game. Sheffield decided then and there he would play along with Wilde. His mind changed as he realized he might have lost her interest. What would make his seduction a more successful attempt was because Wilde would observe. After this, he knew Wilde would improve his game, and then he would have to raise his own stakes. Only, he held a marker in his pocket that Wilde did not. Lord Henry Hartridge, her father. His business relationship with him would be his ace in the hole. Sure, Henry told him Sidney would make the decision on who she would marry. However, he could persuade the man it would be in his best interest to push his claim with Sidney.

Sidney knew she should make small talk with Sheffield, but her mind strayed to Wildeburg. His kiss, his touch, his actions consumed her thoughts. His promise to see her tonight ignited a need she had never felt before. She raised her fingers to her mouth as if she sensed his lips upon hers. Her body shivered in anticipation. Before long, Sheffield shrouded her in his overcoat. Sidney realized he mistook her shiver for cold. Guilt consumed her as she thought of one man while in the presence of another. She glanced toward the trees and wondered if Wildeburg lingered. When she searched for him, she encountered his stare. She sighed. How did she manage to get herself in this mess? Did she wish to be pursued by two empowering men? Was this more than research? What started out as a walk in the park to get her thoughts in order ended with her brain entirely muddled.

Sheffield's overcoat wasn't the only thing to wrap around her shoulders. Before long Sidney became caught in Sheffield's hold, with her hands trapped between their bodies. She tried to push him away from her, but his hold only tightened. When she glanced into his eyes, she witnessed a man bent on victory. As he lowered his head, Sidney turned her head toward the trees, afraid Wildeburg would see their embrace. Why she felt betrayal was unknown to her. She only understood she didn't want him to think her free with her affections. However, Sheffield could not be deterred. He turned her gaze back to him with the simple tilt of his finger on her cheek.

He stroked the smoothness of her cheek until a pink blush stole across her skin. The soft color enhanced the creaminess of her skin. He watched as she searched for Wildeburg. His finger slowly made their way to her full lips. Lips he realized his friend tasted, an advantage soon to be rectified. They trembled under his touch as he ran the tip of his finger back and forth. Her blush became darker as it spread over her entire face.

Sidney stood mortified. While she started her research for this exact outcome, she only held an attraction for one man. And that man was not Sheffield. Oh, at first, she experienced a bit of desire for him. What lady wouldn't? A dashing duke paid her the attention no gentleman ever had, but as soon as Wildeburg's lips touched hers, no man stood a chance. Awkwardness overcame her as Sheffield rubbed his finger across her lips. She cringed on how to discourage his attention without offending him. She needed to be gentle but firm.

The other dilemma was her requirement for the same outcome with her research. She needed each gentleman to kiss her, but now wasn't the place for Sheffield's affection. She planned for them to lure her in the gardens at the Havelock Ball. While Wildeburg had already kissed her, the other two gentlemen must wait for the ball. Then after the event she would finish her research and write her paper. All this silly nonsense would end, and she could resume her normal life helping Papa with his research. She would dress plain again, and the men would withdraw their attentions.

Sidney drew back. "Your Grace, you take liberties that are not allowed."

"Aren't they, my dear? I do not believe I mistook your interest a few days past."

He made a point there. She stroked her hands up and down his chest, as if she was enticing him for a more amorous relationship. Now, she needed to encourage him and discourage him within the same moment. Sidney's mind scrambled for an excuse of her behavior.

"I'm afraid my nature was not the manners of a lady. I hope you don't have an unfair opinion of my behavior?"

"No. It has helped me to finalize a decision."

"A decision?"

"Yes. I have determined you would make an excellent duchess."

She stepped out of his clutches and stood with her mouth open wide. Her eyes grew large as conceit crossed his face at his declaration. He slid his hands in his pockets and stuck out his chest as he arched an eyebrow at her. Sidney believed he thought she should bow before him. Yes, this definitely had moved too far, too fast. What had she done? Sheffield defied all of her research. No offer of marriage was ever to be spoken. They were to take their kisses and leave her to ruination. So far, only one man proved her data to be correct. Sheffield went against all odds and wrecked her research. Which only left Rory, and he would offer for her after a kiss because of his close relationship with her family. She didn't think this through. As usual, she had jumped into a scheme without a thought on how it would play out.

"Are you mad?"

"On the contrary, I am quite sane. I have already spoken with your father, and he has accepted my proposal."

"Proposal? I don't recall you asking for my hand in marriage."

Sheffield scoffed. "Nor will I. Marriage is a business agreement, and nothing more. While I will say your beauty is a draw I never expected from you, it will make bedding you all the more enjoyable. As for your mind, you must rein in your reckless thoughts. I will tolerate them alone, but you will refrain from them in the company of others."

"Why you conceited, overbearing arse."

"Tsk, tsk, my dear. Those are the comments you must learn to abstain from."

"Papa will never agree."

"Yes, you are correct. He has informed me it is your decision to make."

"So, you've decided to persuade me with your arrogant attitude? Yes, I can see you understand how to win a girl's heart."

"Marriage does not involve matters of the heart, dear Sidney."

"I have not given you leave to address me so informally. Also, you are incorrect. The heart is the very soul of a marriage."

"I did not figure someone as level-headed as you are for a romantic. The next thing you will inform me of is your love for romance novels."

"You know that is nonsense, but I know it exists. My father and mother hold a deep love for one another."

"I will agree with you on that subject. Your parents' love is a rare exception. Be honest with yourself. You realize your prospects are not abundant, and you no longer wish to be a burden on your parents. Wouldn't it be a relief to them when you are settled before anything befalls them? A marriage to me would allow your parents comfort and provide your younger siblings with bright futures," he persuaded her.

Sidney listened to his arguments and realized he brought forth good points toward his suit. Wildeburg promised nothing but seduction and only toyed with her affections. The practical side of Sidney recognized the positive points, if she were to encourage Sheffield. Her family would be financially set for the rest of their lives if she wed the duke. Her younger brothers would go to fine schools and have secure futures. The romantic side of Sidney argued that she would be unhappy in a loveless marriage. She wished to allow the attraction with Wildeburg to flourish into a grand love. Her confusion led her to her next comment.

"I will agree to your courtship, Your Grace. After you have proven to be a man I wish to marry, I will agree. Until then, I am free to explore other options if I so desire."

Sheffield stood smug in her acceptance, he now gained a point for himself against Wildeburg. She would be easy to convince. This time, Wildeburg could not outwit him. He would be the victor in the game of Sidney Hartridge. He reached for her gloved hand and raised it to his lips, where he held it for a few seconds, then placed a warm kiss upon her knuckles.

"Agreed. Now, since the rain has halted, may I escort you home? I promised your mother I would."

Not wanting to disappoint her mother, she allowed Sheffield to lay her hand on his arm as he led her down the gazebo steps. The rain stopped as the sun broke through the clouds. The bright rays shone on them as they passed the cluster of trees Wildeburg escaped to. As they passed, she noticed he no longer remained. She suffered disappointment for she had hoped he would interrupt them as he did the time before. But it was not to be.

Sheffield made polite conversation on their short walk home, acting as the ultimate gentleman. He even allowed her to speak her difference of opinion. When they reached her front door, he bowed and thanked her for the lovely walk. Then he turned on his heel and she watched him walk away until he moved out of her view. Nothing more, nothing less, which only left her more confused. She trailed inside, where she told her mama that yes, the duke found her, and yes, they had a lovely chat. She informed her mother she would be in her room reading until lunch.

Chapter Eight

Sidney climbed the steps to her room with her head bent in deep thought. She tried to pull her thoughts together on how to proceed with her research. She already came to the conclusion that she was in way over her head. This afternoon she would list her data into the correct columns and begin to write her paper. After a few days, she would have her outcome. Her footsteps shuffled along the hallway and through the doorway to her room. She shut the door behind her to inform her family and Rose that she didn't wish to be disturbed.

When she raised her head and turned around, she gasped. Wildeburg lay atop her counterpane, with his hands relaxed behind his head. His wicked grin spoke of his true intentions. She gulped as she noted his long form spread across her bed in leisure. He discarded his jacket and a waistcoat on her chaise. He loosened his cravat and left the first few buttons of his shirt open for her to ogle. Lord Wildeburg was a very fine specimen of a man. He rolled on his side with his hand propping his head while he patted the spot next to him.

Her head shook back and forth, since she was unable to utter a single sentence. This was every girl's dream, Noah Wildeburg on their bed. He laughed, then crooked his finger as he tempted her to come closer. As if under his spell, her legs moved toward the bed while her mind screamed, *NO, NO, NO!* It would seem her body had a desire of its own. When she reached him, he lifted his palm, and she slid her hand into his. With a small tug, she soon landed in his arms. Wilde never spoke a word, only lowered his mouth to hers for a kiss.

The kiss, while gentle, held a pressure for release. Each nip and brush of his tongue begged more from her. When she responded as eagerly as him, the pressure of release poured their emotions into the passion. Their kisses became bolder, hungrier for more. Before long, his hands wrapped in her hair, and he drew her closer. The stroke of his tongue guided her to abandon proper restraint. She ran her fingers through his hair, luxuriating in the full honey locks. When his lips moved to her neck, mumbling incoherent words, she pulled his head closer. An ache overcame her body, one that only he could ease. She needed to touch him as he caressed her. When her fingers began unbuttoning the rest of his shirt, he pulled back, enclosing her hand in his. He rested his forehead against hers, breathing deeply. As he stared into her eyes, Sidney watched him try to regain control. She shook her head no.

He closed his eyes as he gathered her closer and held her to his chest as he brought his body under control. Wilde tucked her head into his shoulder, holding her trembling form. She was an enticing minx. He only meant to tease and to gain a reaction to his appearance in her room in broad daylight, not to fall under her spell, but he became lost after one kiss and touch. It was insane, the surest way to end in his demise—marriage. To climb her trellis in the dead of night was one thing, but to climb it during the day only asked for the parson's noose.

When he regarded her in Sheffield's arms, and when she didn't slug his friend, he realized he might have lost the game, which meant he would have had to up his stakes. Wilde didn't want to examine the other emotions he experienced when Sheffield stroked his finger across her cheek. They still lingered for him to process later. At least she didn't grant the bloke a kiss. Of that, he held an advantage. Even though neither of them declared Sidney Hartridge a game, the result was the same. There was nobody and nothing off limits to their level of competition. She was no different, even as delightful of a kisser she was. Not to mention, heaven in his arms. When her body settled into his and her trembles ceased, he breathed a deep sigh.

"When I saw you in Sheffield's arms and he stroked your face, a jealous rage overcame me. I had to see you. Before you lecture me on improprieties, I will apologize. However, I will not say I am sorry for the kiss I stole from your lips."

Sidney raised herself to rest her head on her folded hands as she gazed at him. "My Lord, you are no gentleman. You are the worst scoundrel in all of England."

He released a laugh, sure to draw notice if anybody walked along the hallway. She put her hand over his mouth to quiet him. His tongue stroked the delicate fingers, tasting her. When she moaned and her fingers relaxed under his tongue, he continued the exploration as his mouth moved to her wrist. As his tongue rested against the beating of her rapid pulse, her eyes darkening with heated desire, he decided the hell with Sheffield and their games. He needed to have her.

He raised his head to ravish her lips under his, taking from her what she returned in full. His fingers popped the buttons along the length of her back, with a need to touch and taste her fully. Her moans became lost in his as her fingers slipped inside his shirt to stroke his chest. Sidney's touch set his body aflame, and every coherent thought left his mind. His need only grew stronger. When her lips left to move to his neck, he pressed his hardened cock into her womanly core. As her lips lowered to place soft kisses on his chest, he rotated his hips against hers. He was on the verge of ripping the rest of buttons off her dress when the door flung open. He stilled in horror.

"Sidney, your Mama said you were hiding in your—" Sophia began.

Wilde jumped from the bed and yanked his clothes in order, afraid Sidney's mother would not be far behind. When Lady Sophia closed the door and stood smirking at them, he knew he was safe for the time being. His gaze landed on Sidney, who had also left the bed and set her dress to rights. As her hands tried to smooth her skirts, her head rose to entrance him in her stare. Their unanswered desire sizzled between them, begging for release. He shrugged on his waistcoat and tossed his suit coat over his shoulder and held his hand to her. She moved silently to him and rested her palm in his with complete trust. He glanced over her shoulder to note that Lady Sophia had turned her back on them to offer them a sliver of privacy.

He kissed her forehead. "I will see you tonight," he promised. Wilde tossed his coat out the window and climbed down the trellis as he had the night before.

Sidney watched him exit the garden without being caught by her father. As she turned around, she saw his discarded cravat hanging off her bed. She lifted the blue material to her nose and she sniffed his clean aftershave. When she glanced at Phee, she found her friend at her desk, fanning her face.

"Well I needn't ask how the research is progressing. It would appear you have lured one gentleman into a kiss."

"You misunderstand."

"No, my friend, I haven't."

"Yes, you draw conclusions where there are none to draw."

"You were entwined in a fiery embrace with the most charming rogue of London while he ravished you in your bedchamber; it paints a very clear picture, Sid."

Sidney reclined on her chaise as she wrapped Wilde's cravat around her hand over and over, realizing her friend was correct. He consumed her thoughts with the passion he ignited in her. If Phee hadn't interrupted them, how far would they have gone? Would she have allowed him to make love to her in her bedchamber when someone could have caught them at any moment? She was foolish and didn't need her behavior confirmed. It was a recklessness that held consequences for not only her and Wildeburg, but for her family too. Shame would grace their doorstep. Sidney glanced at Phee, who stared back at her with a confused look she couldn't decipher. The look held one of amusement and pity.

"Phee?"

"Yes."

"I've made such a mess."

"It would appear so."

"What do I do?"

"What do you want to do? Or should I be asking whom?"

"Wildeburg," Sidney sighed.

"Finally."

"Finally?"

"I thought you would never succumb to romance."

"Romance? This emotion is beyond romance."

"Then for once in your life don't analyze your feelings. Explore them."

"But what if his intentions are to toy with me?"

"What if they aren't?"

"Am I crazy?"

"No, Sid, you are a woman being awoken to desire."

"Sheffield claimed his intentions were for marriage this morning. He has declared to Papa his suit and forms strong claims to our union."

Sophia came off her chair and knelt in front of Sidney as she drew her hands into hers. "You cannot marry that conceited arse. He would be the biggest mistake of your life. Promise me you will not tie yourself to him. Give Wildeburg a chance."

"Sheffield provided good points for our union. Mama and Papa would never worry about money, and the boys would have bright futures."

"Do not sacrifice yourself for status. Your family wouldn't expect it from you. Sheffield is only planting ideas inside your head."

"You warned me, and I didn't listen."

"You never do, that is what makes being your friend so adventurous. Now give me details. I want to know if kissing Lord Wildeburg is as delightful as it looked."

"Even more so," Sidney sighed.

"When are you seeing him again?"

"Tonight, at the Steadhampton Musical."

"Perfect. I will run interference with your other suitors while you two sneak away for some private moments. But Sidney, you must be careful you don't get caught."

"I only need a few moments with him to inform him he needs to court me properly for our acquaintance to continue. If he is interested in me for more than my body, then he will agree. If not, then he isn't the one for me. I need to know his true intentions."

Sophia agreed with her, then she let the subject drop. She could tell Sidney's thoughts were troubled and that she needed to process her emotions on her own. She continued to hold her hand as her friend's eyes drifted away, lost in reflection. While she wished to know more of what transpired before she interrupted them, she understood that they were private memories Sidney wished to keep to herself. Phee took absolute delight in the scene she walked in on and knew without a doubt Lord Wildeburg was just the man to lead her friend on a romantic journey.

It was not long before Mama and Rose invaded her room. They bustled in with a new dress of Phee's they hemmed for her, declaring how gorgeous she would look tonight.

"What are you twirling around in your hand, dear?" her mother inquired.

Sidney's eyes widened at her mother's question. Sophia acted quick on her feet when she grabbed the fabric and shoved it inside her pocket.

"Only a piece of fabric I plan on using for a blanket I am making for Mama. Please keep my secret. It is a surprise for her birthday."

"You are a dear girl, Sophia. Mum's the word. I cannot wait to see the finished product. From what I saw, it was a lovely shade of blue."

Sidney rose from the chaise in panic but calmed when her friend covered for her. Her antics would soon draw her mother's full attention. But it seemed, after she skirted one issue, another soon arose when Rose saw the state of her undress and the missing buttons from her dress.

"It was if someone ripped the garment from your body. This will take me the entire evening to repair."

Her mother frowned at her state of undress. A man's cravat and ripped clothing sent Sidney into a panic as she noticed the messed bed sheets. Soon, her mother would add all the evidence together and come to a conclusion that would end her research. She shot her eyes to Phee and motioned with her eyes toward the bed. Her friend realized her dilemma and threw herself on the bed to muss the cover more.

"That was all my fault, Lady Hartridge. I told Sid about the dress you fixed and was eager for her to try it on. In my excitement, I popped a few buttons lose. Someone hooked them so tight, I pulled, and then *poof*, they sprang apart."

"Well, that is all right dear. To be honest, this rag needs to retire to the dustbin. I'm ashamed the Duke of Sheffield witnessed you in this monstrosity. The horror. What must he think of our family?"

"Mama, there is no need to be ashamed. I hardly think Sheffield took any notice of my apparel today. His mind was otherwise occupied." She wrapped Mama in a hug while she whispered a thank you to Phee over her mother's shoulder.

Phee lay on the bed with a mischievous grin on her face while she picked up the pearl-seeded buttons scattered across the counterpane. After she finished, she wandered to Sid's desk, where she slid the buttons and cravat into her secret drawer. By then, Sidney's mother and Rose had removed her clothes and prepared her for the evening. Phee crossed to her side and kissed her on the cheek in good-bye, with a promise to see her later at the musical.

~~~~~~

Sidney waited at the entryway to the music room as she searched for him. He had not shown his face yet, and no mention of him amongst the guests meant he wasn't present. A throng of people entered the room, for the concert was set to start soon. She stood on her tiptoes to look above the gentlemen's heads, as they obscured her view of the door. Soon her mother was upon her and urged her to take her seat.

"I will be along shortly, Mama. I am waiting for Sophia."

"Well, don't be long, dear. Sheffield is saving our seats."

"I promise." Sidney grimaced at the thought of being stuck in the duke's company for the evening.

Sophia soon rushed to her side with her mother. Phee promised her mother they would be in soon as she noticed Sidney's attention focused on the door. She had a notion whom she waited for. When the last of the guests trickled inside, Sidney's eyes took on a dejected expression.

"Perhaps he is running late."

"Or he decided not to appear after all."

"Who will not appear this evening?" Rory asked over their shoulders.

"A friend," Sophia replied.

"Which friend?"

"We should take our seats; the musical is about to start." Sophia tried to direct them into the music room to conceal Sidney's questionable behavior from Rory.

Sophia was unable to direct them inside before Sheffield came upon them. He positioned himself next to Sidney as he displayed his dominance over Rory. Sophia narrowed her eyes at his domineering behavior. Phee would not allow him to win over Sidney. She made a promise to herself that Sidney would find love, and Sheffield wasn't the man.

"Your Grace, I notice you're missing your sidekick this evening," Sophia said.

"Ah, Wildeburg. I'm afraid he had a previous engagement with Madame Bellerose."

"Madame Bellerose?" Sidney questioned.

"Now, Sheffield, these ladies should not be subjected to this discussion," Rory interjected. He reached for Sidney's arm, disgusted with Sheffield's comments.

Sheffield stood with a smirk of satisfaction. He managed to lay doubt in Lady Sidney's mind about Wildeburg. Also, he knew between her and Lady Sophia they would wiggle Madame Bellerose's identity from Lord Beckwith. While he was not a good friend to Beckwith, he admired the man and his intellect. He also spotted him as competition. His protective behavior didn't go unnoticed as he watched Rory escort Lady Sidney to her mother.

He proceeded to follow them when he heard a *humph* next to him. When he glanced to his right, he observed Lady Sophia with her arms crossed, glaring at him. Her feet beat a fast rhythm as she tried to keep her temper under control. His interest did not lie with her, but she portrayed a fetching piece when riled. Her blonde hair was piled high on her head, displaying her creamy neck, where ear bobs dangled as she shook her head. Her violet eyes shot daggers in his direction. Violet? Were her eyes really purple? He stepped closer to her to discover. When he brought himself within a few inches, he found they were. A dark amethyst that became darker as he peered into them. He felt her breath fan out across his lips as he continued to gaze into her eyes. They were fascinating to him. When she pressed her hand against his chest to push him away, he shook himself out from under her spell.

"Who is this Madame Bellerose?"

"A lady of ill repute."

"Why were you so cruel to mention her to Sidney?"

"Sometimes you must use cruelty to prevent heartache. I can understand Lady Sidney's draw to Lord Wildeburg's charm, but it can only end badly."

"You cannot control them."

"Oh, but I can, and I will. I am a duke, and I have chosen her for my bride, and that is how it will be."

"You are a pompous man."

"You are allowed your opinion. But let me send you a warning. Nobody—and that includes you—will stand in my way. So, tread softly, My Lady."

The lights dimmed as the concert began. He offered his arm because he knew she would take it. For her to snub a duke would be the end to her current season and any season in the future. She slid her palm over his arm, and her fingers gripped him in frustration, which only made his smug smile grow wider. Her perfume swirled around them as they threaded their way to their seats. The only two remaining seats in their party were seated together. It would seem he must endure the concert surrounded by her anger. Well, he found it delightful, and he had succeeded in tarnishing Wilde's name. He relaxed into his seat and divided his attention between the ladies.

"Who is Madame Bellerose?" Sidney whispered to Rory from behind her fan.

"Nobody you need to be aware of."

"Please tell me, Rory. I must know."

"No."

Sidney lowered her fan and closed it to squeeze between her hands. Sadness invaded her soul when she realized she wouldn't see Wildeburg this evening. Her anger grew when Sheffield informed her of Wilde's current amusement. Then Rory attempted to keep her in the dark. She'd about had it with him. His brotherly concern annoyed her.

Rory sensed Sidney's anger. He witnessed it multiple times before and knew enough to know they were about to come upon a storm if he didn't calm her. He laid his hand over hers and loosened the fan from her grip. When she released the fan, he patted her hands to calm her. To his relief, her grasp relaxed, and she rested her palms on her skirts. As she turned her tear-filled gaze to him, he became lost in their sorrow. It was then he realized he had no chance with her, but that the other two gentlemen didn't deserve her affections either. As long as they would pursue her, then so would he. So, for her best interests, he continued what Sheffield started. He slandered Wildeburg in her eyes.

"Madame Bellerose is the most sought after madame in all of London. She runs a brothel of the highest esteem for gentlemen in the aristocracy. Wildeburg is a frequent customer of hers, so I have heard."

Sidney shook her head in denial to his claim. He answered with a nod of his head in the affirmative. She glanced over her shoulder to Phee, who regarded her with a look of sympathy. When she noticed the smugness covering Sheffield's face, she felt betrayal seep into her heart. Sheffield's looked also displayed his determination to make her his bride. When he arched his eyebrow at her, she turned back in her seat. Sidney couldn't tell you about the concert performance, for she sat twisting her hands in her lap as she tried to control her emotions.

Why, after the affections he bestowed on her the night before and throughout the day, did he betray her with a visit to a brothel? Did he toy with her emotions as part of a game? While her heart screamed no, her mind informed her yes. Wildeburg's dalliances were well-known throughout the ton, and she had just fallen victim to his wicked charm. When the singer sang a sorrowful passage, Sidney's bruised heart cried. Silent tears flowed inside as her dreams of romance died on the final notes. As she stood to applaud the concert, her heart hardened, and her mind became determined to finish her research, exposing all the men and their games to the female heart.

When the concert ended, both men tried to push their way to her side to escort her around the room. She evaded them and pulled Phee into an empty room. They slipped inside the dark parlor, and Sidney sank onto the sofa.

"He preferred a brothel to my boring company."

"You are never boring, my friend."

"Why did I imagine I could intrigue a man of Wildeburg's esteem?"

"He could only be so lucky for your attention."

"I was a fool."

Sophia rested beside her and drew her into her arms. "He was the fool, Sid."

Sidney shed the tears she held inside herself during the concert. Wet drops slid along her face as her friend comforted her. Sophia's soft words helped to bolster her tattered ego. When she regained control over her emotions, she sighed and rested her head on Phee's shoulder. Neither one of them discussed Wildeburg, each confused with the gentleman's behavior. Sophia reached into her reticule and handed Sid a handkerchief. Sid wiped her eyes and handed the garment back to Phee. She pasted a grin on her face and hugged her friend.

"Onward and upward, Phee."

When Sidney uttered those words, Phee knew it was hopeless to persuade her with a list of excuses for Wildeburg's absence. She already moved on, and it would be pointless to convince her of the marquess's innocence, especially when she wasn't convinced herself. He was a rogue who played a part in convincing her how to lure her friend into his charm. She was partly to blame for Sidney's disappointment and felt an extreme sense of guilt.

"I'm sorry, Sidney."

"You have nothing to apologize for. It's my own fault I fell for his charm."

"But I helped him."

"Nonsense, you fell for his charm too. Only he conned you into helping his bid along."

"But—"

"But nothing. We are finished with the subject of Lord Noah Wildeburg. He is only to be mentioned as a subject for my research. After the Havelock Ball, he will no longer be a thought in our heads. I will take my revenge on him soon enough."

Sidney rose from the couch and held her hand for Phee. Together they made their way to their mothers' sides. As they made small talk for the remainder of the event, Sidney was well aware of the curious glances Rory and Sheffield settled on her.

Neither man pressed their suit this evening, both aware of her vulnerable feelings. While it would be the perfect time for them to strike on their advances, both men understood her temper and didn't want it projected amongst themselves. Tomorrow would be the earliest time to continue their pursuits.

~~~~~

For all of her arguments with Phee on the removal of Lord Wildeburg from her mind, they were nothing but brave words to soothe her ego. As she sat at her desk taking notes, she waited for him. Every whistle of the wind or tree branch scraping her window brought her to her feet, anxiously waiting for him to climb into her bedchamber. When the hour grew late, drawing into the wee hours of the early morning, Sidney finally faced the fact that he wouldn't appear. She blew out her light and wandered to the window, where she pulled the drapes back to peer into the garden. As she looked outside, the moon rose high in the sky with the stars shooting light into the garden. There was still no sign of Wildeburg. She glanced to the bench where he offered her candy, only to find it empty. She sighed and crawled under the covers. As she stared at the ceiling, a sense of loss invaded her soul. A loss she couldn't understand, for it was a loss of the unknown. Still it saddened her. She rolled on her side and closed her eyes as exhaustion took hold. As she drifted to sleep, tears rolled onto her pillow, soaking into her hair.

~~~~~~

He watched her bedchamber from the alleyway behind her house for hours. He waited for her light to extinguish, but it never did. Wilde failed her this evening and knew, without a doubt, he had lost his chance with her. When her room was shrouded in darkness, he noticed her curtains open. Her silhouette appeared before the window as she searched the garden. Did she hope to find him there? She only waited for a moment, but it was long enough for him to decide she was worth the fight. Sidney held a goodness to her that he didn't deserve but wanted to explore.

Wilde discovered this evening the depth of his need to conquer. After he located Sheffield at White's, he discovered how far his friend went to slander his good name with the lady. When he came upon his friend, he found him sharing a drink with Rory Beckwith. Wilde's suspicions grew when he joined their party because the two men rarely ran in the same circles. The smug smile of victory that graced Sheffield's face was nothing compared to the glare from Beckwith. The man appeared ready to leap from his chair and slug him. He narrowed his eyes back at Beckwith, and then at Sheffield. Something was amiss, and it pointed toward Wilde.

"Bugger off, Beckwith. I need to have a private word with Sheffield."

"Not until I discuss your involvement with Sidney."

"Sidney who?" Wildeburg questioned while not taking his eyes off of Alex.

"Lady Sidney Hartridge," Rory growled as he advanced on Wildeburg.

Wilde turned his head toward Beckwith, pretending indifference of the subject being discussed. "And who is she again?"

"Why, you ..." Rory gritted his teeth as he grabbed Wilde by the lapels of his suit.

By this time, every member inside the club gathered around them hoping to witness a fight. Soon, bets rang out, with Beckwith in the favor. Every gentleman of the ton knew of his temper and the strength of his fists. A good deal of them wanted revenge against Wildeburg for the attention he paid to their wives or daughters. Nobody knew yet of the reason for their altercation, and they didn't care. It would be a source of entertainment for a dull evening.

Sheffield rose and separated the pair. He pushed Wilde into a leather chair near the fire while he whispered to Rory a promise to take care of their problem. With one last furious glance at Wildeburg, Rory strode out of the club while the patrons moaned their disappointment in the background. They questioned Beckwith as he exited, but he swatted their questions away in annoyance. Not only were the men out of watching a scuffle, they had no gossip to spread with their wives or mistresses. Sheffield waved the server over to bring Wilde a drink. Once the waiter filled their glasses, Sheffield lifted his whiskey in a toast to his friend.

"You sure know how to make enemies, my friend. Pretending ignorance of the young lady will not gain you any favors."

"Where were you tonight? Belle needed your assistance."

"Did you help her?"

"Yes, but that is not the point. Your friend required your help."

"I am aware of her needs, and that is the reason I sent for you to remove her problem. Since you succeeded, all is well."

Wilde nursed his drink as he watched Sheffield's disinterest about Belle's troubles. Any other time, Alex would have risen to the occasion to help her, but this time he pawned it off on him to rescue her. He didn't mind rescuing Belle, but he did mind the underhanded techniques used to prevent him from attending the Steadhampton Musical. A sense of doom overcame him as he realized his non-appearance resulted in his loss of Sidney. Why else would her friend Beckwith confront him in anger? His glance at Alex confirmed his suspicions. A man as confident as Sheffield sat relaxed as he drank his whiskey. He was a man who appeared victorious in an accomplished game of winning the hand of a lady by underhanded means.

"How was the musical?"

"Most enlightening, I must say."

"How so?"

"Lady Sidney attended with her barracuda of a friend Lady Sophia."

"I find Lady Sophia to be enchanting."

"Yes, well, maybe you might have luck with her then, since Lady Sidney is quite disenchanted with you after this evening."

"And why would that be?"

"Somehow, she heard the rumors of your visitation to Belle's and what type of establishment you frequent."

"Who would burn her ears with such gossip?"

"Who else?"

"This is far from over, Alex. I never thought you would slander your own friend for a chit, especially with a false rumor. You were fully aware of the reason for my visit to Belle's. Hell you sent me there."

"I have decided Lady Sidney will be my duchess, and I mean to secure her. Your secret meetings with her will end now. I don't want to lose our friendship, but if you continue your liaisons with her, you will leave me with no choice but to ruin you."

Wilde stood and straightened his suit jacket, tugging on the sleeves. "Well consider myself ruined. If you wish to discard our friendship so easily, then prepare yourself for a fight. You see, I aim to make her my marchioness. May the best man win." He took a bow before Sheffield and wandered from the club, his whistle growing louder as he left.

~~~~~

He loosened his fists as he controlled his anger. Wilde wanted to punch the pompous look from Sheffield's face but realized it would have been of no use. Alex changed the rules of the game tonight.

He either backed away from Sidney, or Sheffield would ruin him. It no longer mattered. His feelings for this lady were on another level, which would lead him on a path to happiness or despair.

Once she disappeared from the window, he let himself in through the garden gate and continued toward the bench. He glanced to her window again and wished for her to call out to him. When she didn't, he laid a token of his apology to her on the bench, hoping she would discover it in the morning. He took another glance before he left for home. He would need to rise early, to stay one step ahead of Sheffield and any other gentleman who would call on her tomorrow. Sidney was no longer a game to him, but a challenge of love.

Chapter Nine

As Sidney trailed listlessly along the hallway toward the library, her footsteps halted as she heard her mother gush over a guest. A male voice drifted from the parlor in a low muffled voice. When her mother released a loud giggle, joined by Sophia's melodious laugh, Sidney's steps gathered speed as she rushed into the room. She stopped when she found her mother and Phee on the sofa, across from Lord Wildeburg, who sat in her father's favorite armchair. He lounged in the chair as if he had countless times before and laughed along with the ladies.

When he noticed her, he leaped to his feet and flashed a flirtatious smile her way. In return, Sidney glared at him. However, her scowl only made his smile grow wider, if possible. As his smile grew, the twinkle in his eye revealed his amusement at her temper. He approached and offered his arm as he led her to the chair near the couch. The audacity of him to show his face in her home, where he knew she would not welcome him, infuriated her. As he returned to his seat, Sid felt the loss of his touch deeply. He only held her hands for a few seconds, but it felt as if it were for an eternity. Her attraction to him overruled her anger, which was something she needed to squash if she were to stay impartial on her thesis. Her glance slid to the sofa. Her mother smiled with glee at the marquess, while her friend looked guilty for consorting with the enemy. It would appear as if it would rest upon her to rid the marquess of their company. She didn't want to draw suspicion to her mother by displaying rude behavior, but he must leave. He wreaked havoc with her emotions.

"Lady Sidney, you look lovely this sunny day," he flattered her.

"Thank you, My Lord."

"I wondered if you would do me the honor of taking a walk this afternoon?"

"I am sorry. I am otherwise occupied. Perhaps another time."

"Nonsense, you must accompany Lord Wildeburg since he took time from his busy schedule to pay us a visit today. He informed me of his wish to spend time with you but has been unable to because of your other suitors. Today would be a perfect day for you to get to know the charming marquess," her mother cajoled her.

Sidney turned her head and tilted it to the side as she regarded Wildeburg. Her eyes narrowed in suspicion. When he sent a wink in her direction, she wanted to confess to her mother the many opportunities he had spent in her company. He knew she couldn't reveal their moments together without ruining herself. She would be the one at fault, not him, which only infuriated her more and proved her thesis. The devil would play on her virtue for his own gain.

When Rory arrived in the doorway, she realized he would be her salvation. He took notice of the room and its occupants. The two ladies on the sofa sat charmed by the marquess, while Sidney glowered at the man, expressing her anger with him. When her eyes landed on Rory, she rose from the seat and sent him a silent message with her eyes to play along with her. Rory nodded as he sensed the vibe in the room.

"Mama, I cannot join Lord Wildeburg, as I have promised Rory a walk around the garden."

"My loss, your gain, Beckwith. Lady Sidney I will feel the loss of your presence deeply. I hope you enjoy your stroll. Lady Hartridge and Lady Sophia, it has been a pleasure to share tea with you this afternoon."

"We can't make your visit go unnoticed. Perhaps you would enjoy a walk with Lady Sophia instead?"

"I would be honored if Lady Sophia accompanied me to the park nearby."

Lady Hartridge placed Sophia in an awkward position, one where she either offended a peer of the realm or betray her best friend. Lady Hartridge, unaware of the tension floating around the room, sent an elbow into her side for her to rise and take the arm Lord Wildeburg offered. As she rose, she laid her arm on his, and he walked them to the doorway. Sidney and Rory blocked their path, as they both glared their frustration at the marquess's manipulation. Only Wilde hadn't manipulated the situation, Lady Hartridge had. Sidney's mother would never have made the offer if Lord Wildeburg hadn't shown his face at the Hartridges' home today. When Sophia's eyes met Sidney's she expected anger. Instead, she watched tears gather in her eyes. She took a step forward when Sid shook her head in denial and stepped to the side for them to exit.

"Make your excuses, Wildeburg, and leave these ladies in peace," Rory growled low.

"Enjoy your walk, Sophia," Sidney said.

"Good day, Lady Sidney. Beckwith," Wildeburg replied as he escorted Sophia along the hallway to the front door.

Sidney turned and stalked in the opposite direction, with Rory following in her wake. She pushed open the French doors leading outside and rushed into the garden. Usually the garden's peaceful nature settled her troubled emotions, but not today. He had ruined the tranquility of the garden for her too. Every turn she made, he was there. From the trellis climbing the house, to the spot in the garden under her window. She slowly turned in a circle as she tried to erase him from her heart. When her eyes settled on the bench he occupied a few days ago, she realized without a doubt it was worthless to remove him from her mind.

As she drifted toward the pull of the empty bench, she spotted a small object resting on the planks. She bent over and lifted a small bottle of perfume with a piece of butterscotch candy hanging from the ribbon. The bottle, wet from the morning dew, proved he visited during the night. He had come for her. Now, she was more confused than ever. Perhaps Sheffield was mistaken on Wildeburg's whereabouts the previous evening and spoke falsely. His unspoken apology soothed her battered emotions.

"Sidney, we must talk."

"Not now Rory, I must …" Sidney slid the bottle into her pocket as she kept the gift from his eyes.

"You must what?"

"What?"

"Exactly, you stated we couldn't talk because you must …"

"What must I do?"

"That is what I asked you?"

"You are confusing me, Rory. Now if you will excuse me, I need to—"

"No, I will not excuse you, Sidney Hartridge. You must listen this instant."

Sidney, taken aback by his authoritative behavior, paused. This wasn't Rory's normal attitude with her. He was always friendly and protective, not a bully. She then realized her unfair treatment of her friend and her need to apologize to him. As she took a seat on the bench, she patted the space next to her. Rory ran his hand through his hair in his frustration with her. His red locks turned brighter as the sun beat upon his head. Tiny flecks of gold glistened in between his dark locks. He was quite handsome to gaze upon, if you admired a rough look. Her friend settled next to her with a deep sigh. Sidney didn't understand his frustrations, so she slid her palm inside his.

"What is it you wish to discuss, Rory?"

"Wildeburg."

"What of Lord Wildeburg?"

"He is not the gentleman for you. You play with fire if you interact with him—and Sheffield for that matter. They will eat you up and spit you out, all for a game they like to play."

"Nonsense. They are harmless. Perhaps I play a game with them."

"Either way, I don't wish any harm on you."

"You know I can take care of myself."

"At one time, yes. But anymore, I am unsure. You have changed into a lady I have never had the opportunity to understand."

"You are talking in riddles, Rory."

"Am I?"

"I am the same. Nothing about my personality has changed."

"All the more reason to be cautious. You are unaware of your own vulnerability. Please heed my advice and beware."

"How have I changed?"

"You have become softer."

"How so?"

Rory smiled wistfully at her. "By becoming lost in yourself because of the false flattery the gentlemen of the aristocracy are famous for. I always figured you to be immune to their charms."

"I still am. I realize their compliments are false."

"Then please help me understand why your expression takes on a dreamy quality when Wildeburg is near you."

"You speak nonsense."

"Do I?" He let the question hang in the air between them as he rose.

"Thank you for rescuing me earlier."

"It was my pleasure. Please err on the side of caution and end this farce."

"I will in a few days' time."

"What will happen then?"

"You will know soon enough."

Rory shook his head at her antics as he wandered into the house. Rory was a standing guest in their home during the day. His close association with her father's research enabled him free rein. Her parents trusted them to be alone together, for they displayed nothing more than a friendship. His flirtatious behavior disappeared back into their relaxed companionship.

Sidney remained in the garden, awaiting the return of Sophia. They were to discuss Sidney's attire for the ball. She wanted to wear a piece to make every gentleman stand and take notice on the last night of her research. Her appearance needed to make every man tempt her into the garden, Rory included. She took the vial of perfume out of her pocket and slid off the topper. When she lifted the bottle to her nose, a field full of lilies drifted across her senses. The light scent tugged at her heart He knew her perfume without asking her.

She imagined different scenarios if she had seen him the night before in the garden.

~~~~~

"You hurt her with your absence at the musical."

"I know, but a dear friend was in need of assistance, and I couldn't refuse."

"Is that what you use for an explanation to visit a brothel? Really, whenever you do get married, you will need a better excuse."

Wildeburg sighed his frustration. "Perhaps I can explain."

"Please try. I want to plead your case to Sidney, but I am unable when you have hurt her."

Wildeburg led Lady Sophia to a park bench and explained his reason for missing the musical. He also apologized for the sensitive nature of his excuse. When Belle sent for Sheffield to remove an overzealous earl from her establishment, the duke refused and sent for Wildeburg to clean up the mess. When he arrived at Belle's, he found her girls in terror as a drunken earl brandished a knife. He threatened to cut the girl who exposed him to his father-in-law. The gentleman already beat a girl and left her frightened of her own shadow before he arrived. With the help of Belle's bodyguards, they disarmed the man and escorted him from the premises.

Belle hoped Sheffield's influence would frighten the man out of his shameful behavior. When Wilde appeared instead, it fueled the earl's anger. For Wilde was known to have tasted the charms of the earl's wife. A false claim, but one spread all the same after the wife discovered her husband's love of brothels. Who else to enflame her husband's anger than to whisper a rumor of an entangled affair with the charmer of the ton. He swore his innocence to Lady Sophia and hoped she believed him. When he knocked out the earl, he directed Belle's bodyguards to deliver him to his wife's father, the Duke of Marwood. The duke could handle the rest of his son-in-law's mess.

He then calmed Belle and her girls by turning away any possible business for the night. It was late when he finished, too late to apologize. He didn't discuss his jaunt to White's and Sheffield's smugness, or of his visit to Sidney's garden. He hoped his story would clear any misconceptions regarding his character.

"Why didn't Sheffield answer her summons?"

"I can only assume he meant to smear me in Lady Sidney's eyes and keep me from her."

"Yes, he displayed his arrogance as he disclosed your whereabouts. The conceited arse."

Wilde laughed at her amusing description of Sheffield. "Can you explain my innocence?"

"Oh, leave Sidney in my hands. For that matter, leave Sheffield to me too. I cannot stand the man, but I will suffer through his company as I keep him from her."

"You, my dear, are a priceless friend."

Sophia waved his compliment away as she pressed her next question. "What of the girl, the one who the earl beat?"

"She will recover in a cottage outside of London."

"Then will she have to …"

"No, someone has offered her a stipend to help her establish a new life."

"Courtesy of you?"

"I cannot say."

"Mmm, your silence is answer enough for me."

"What is the next event Sidney will attend?"

"The Havelock Ball."

"Perfect. Can I assume you will lend me your help so I can have a few moments alone with Sidney?"

"You may."

"Excellent. Now, I believe we should return."

"I agree. Before you return me to Sidney, I want to tell you that your friendship enlightens me toward your care of others less fortunate than yourself."

Wildeburg tipped his head as he acknowledged her praise. On their way to the Hartridge residence, they discussed small non-trivial matters. Instead of discussing Sidney, he inquired of Sophia's interests and desires. Their talk formed a friendship, which was new for Wilde. He'd never had a female friend, except for Belle, so he supposed his character was evolving.

~~~~~~

Sophia raced up the stairs into Sidney's bedchamber. She found her friend staring at a glass of perfume in the middle of her desk. She hoped to erase the troubled look on her face with her news of Lord Wildeburg. Phee understood her friend's disappointment with his absence from the musical. However, she also hoped to change Sidney's mind after she shared his story. When her friend didn't raise her head at her arrival, she knelt to grab Sidney's hand.

"What is it, Sid?"

"A bottle of perfume."

"A new fragrance to try?"

"No, it is the same kind I always wear."

"Lilies?"

"Yes. Did you tell him my scent?"

"No, Sid, I swear I did not," Sophia exclaimed, crossing her heart as Sidney gave her a suspicious stare.

"Mmm," Sidney murmured.

"Sid?"

"It doesn't matter anyway. He's revealed his philandering ways. He remains a subject, nothing more. This display of persuasion is a false token, one to draw me into a web of ruin. We shall see about that, Lord Wildeburg."

"You are wrong, Sid. I believe the gift to be sincere. He explained the reason behind his whereabouts last night."

"More lies, Phee. The man will charm his way out of any bad situation to make himself appear the victim."

"No. Unfortunately, another person was a victim of last night's situation, not him. However, he brought the action to a close when he saved others from being hurt. The injustice those women have to suffer to earn a living saddens me. No, last night he showed his true friendship to another, while the swine Sheffield used the opportunity to advance his game of winning your hand. The despicable duke needs to be taken down a peg or two, and I have decided I am the lady for the task."

"Explain yourself, Phee. You have lost me. How does Wildeburg turn into the hero and Sheffield the villain?"

Phee explained to Sidney the exact story from Wildeburg's description, word for word. She elaborated on Wilde's heroism to help her new friend regain Sidney's affections. When Sidney's expression changed throughout the story, Phee realized she had reached through to her.

"How awful for those women. Even they aren't safe from the scoundrels of the ton. Is any lady safe? I must meet Belle and learn these women's stories. I can add their information to my research."

"Sidney, you can't. That is taking your research too far. We cannot meet these women."

"Wildeburg can introduce us."

"No, I'm stopping this. I should have ended this research as soon as you suggested it. Don't make me go to your mother on this."

"You are an accomplice now, Phee. You must see this through to the end alongside me."

Sidney rose from the desk and slid on her pelisse. As she grabbed her reticule, she turned at the door. "Are you coming with me? We will have to tell Mama a little lie about heading to your house to look through your dresses."

"She will want to accompany us and visit Mama."

"Not today. She is attending a hospital committee meeting at Lady's Darvel's house. Your Mama won't go anywhere near there."

Sophia groaned. Sidney was correct. Mama wouldn't step foot on Lady Darvel's doorstep. She would accompany Sid to keep her from trouble, but after this, the Havelock Ball couldn't come soon enough. This visit could be their ruination, but her desire to learn more about these women and their lives tempted her to follow her friend. If Sophia could help these women to a better life, then she must learn more.

"If trouble arises for any reason, you must promise me we will leave immediately."

"I promise." Sidney smiled her satisfaction as she grabbed Phee's hand and laughed her way down the stairs.

Chapter Ten

Through gentle persuasion and a small bribe, Sidney acquired the address to the madame's house through her father's driver and footman. They were in her debt after she found them playing a card game a few weeks ago. Sidney's father loathed gambling in any form and expected his servants to abide by his standards. When she discovered their entertainment, she convinced them to let her play, and she had won every hand. Instead of taking their money, she extracted promises from them. They agreed to keep silent whenever she needed a favor. So, with directions to their destination and guards to protect them, she and Phee set off for the infamous Belle's.

Sidney rode in silence as she pondered Wilde's innocence and the questions she wished to ask Madame Bellerose. Since he convinced Phee to plead his case, would he appear this evening? Sidney hoped so. She daydreamed of her acceptance if he should sneak into her bedroom. She would welcome his attentions with an open heart. Of course, she wouldn't make it easy for him. He must work his charm on her affections. Sidney smiled in anticipation. Sophia's huge sigh and the tapping of her foot interrupted her musings. When her friend became agitated, she would tap her foot until she calmed herself. Sidney reached to set her hand on Phee's knee, giving it a reassuring squeeze.

"I can have Landers drive you home as soon as we arrive. I will stop by on my way home and fill you in on what I have learned."

Phee stilled her leg and shook her head in refusal. "No, I only want to state my objections for the record. Our visit to Madame Belle's is a horrible idea, and we shall be ruined from this, mark my words."

"Nonsense, Phee. I have already made arrangements with Landers. He will stop near the door and drive the carriage to the alleyway to await our departure. From what I understand, ladies arrive for tea every day. The gentlemen have more discretion and arrive at the back door throughout the evening. We shall be in and out of Madame Belle's and home before the sun sets. Nobody will be the wiser."

By then, the conveyance had come to a stop, and Sidney's footman ushered the ladies to the front door. He rang the bell and swiftly returned to the carriage, where Landers drove them around the corner and out of sight. When the door opened, an enormous man with bulging muscles inquired about their business. Sidney stuttered a reply, which drew a frown from the giant. Her fear kept her from remembering what she muttered. Now she understood her friend's anxiety of the unknown. What did she walk them into?

As she grabbed Phee by the arm and started to guide her backward toward the door, an elegant woman appeared next to the man. If the giant scared her, the woman made her feel inadequate as a female. Her long red hair trailed along, clinging to her curvaceous body. Her dress, while it appeared demure and fashionable for the day, was anything but on her form. The woman undid a few small buttons, so she could fold the fabric open to display her ample breasts. The simple linen dress molded tightly to her small frame. Sidney gulped as the lady smiled in welcome. Her nerves kept her from speaking to the enchanting creature. If this beauty was Belle, then Sidney imagined the other girls were gorgeous too.

"You young ladies must be lost. I will have Ned locate a carriage to take you home," the enchantress spoke.

"I hope we are not lost. I seek a woman named Belle," Sidney stuttered.

"I am Belle; however, it would be in your best interests to leave."

"I only wish a few moments of your time. I understand Lord Wildeburg—"

"Wildeburg?" Belle interrupted.

"Yes, as I was saying, Lord Wilde—"

"Ned, please show these young ladies to my parlor. If you would be so kind as to follow Ned, I will be along shortly," Belle said.

Before either one of them could speak, the giant shuffled them into a grand parlor, one fit for a duchess. Most would expect a tawdry parlor decorated in scarlet, not one in various shades of cream. Each elegant fixture enhanced the inviting chamber, especially the drapes made from Chinese silk. The furniture was carved with the finest craftmanship, sitting them in a comfort they did not expect. The personal touches to the room enticed Sidney's curiosity to a new level. The room held picture frames scattered across the fireplace ledge, and small trinkets rested amongst vases of flowers. What captivated the most wonderment was the massive display of books along one wall. Sidney wandered to the books to scan the various degrees of literature. The books ranged from the recent gothic novels to history tomes of undiscovered civilizations. This wasn't the parlor of a brothel owner, but of a lady of mystery. Who was Madame Bellerose?

"What a gorgeous room," Sophia exclaimed in awe.

Before Sidney could reply with the same sentiments, Madame Belle followed a servant, laden with a tea tray and refreshments, inside the room. After the maid poured the beverage, the madame dismissed her.

Belle waited for the maid to leave before she addressed the ladies who sat before her. As she observed them over the rim of her cup, she reached a decision on who captured Wildeburg's heart. The lady was exquisite and seemed the perfect match for her friend. With her auburn hair pulled in a bun, she appeared dowdy in her dress, but Belle recognized the true beauty beneath the disguise. Of all the years spent in her profession, she could spot a temptress right away. This lovely creature would ensnare a man with Wilde's appetites with utter devotion. The young woman held confidence and complete ease in the company of a well-known madame. Belle chuckled to herself at the demise of her friend's bachelorhood.

The other young lady appeared nervous in her presence and kept an eye on the door, in fear of being discovered in a brothel. She was a beauty herself, who wasn't afraid to show her attributes. She was the picture of a prim and proper virgin. The ultimate English rose, with her blond hair flawlessly arranged under her bonnet. Her dress was designed in the latest fashion, and not a ruffle was out of place. Yet, the young miss displayed a curiosity for her home. Belle watched as her gaze held a respect for her parlor—and for Belle herself. She became entranced in the lady's amazing eye color. A rich vibrant violet caught her gaze as she admired Belle's clothing. Belle dressed for comfort today after the tiring events of the evening before. The brothel remained closed for a few hours as her girls comforted one another. If the lady was enamored of this ensemble, those purple eyes would hold shock at the more elaborate designs she wore.

"You mentioned earlier your acquaintance with Lord Wildeburg," Belle inquired.

"Yes, I understand he came to your assistance last night. Is this correct?" Sidney replied.

"He took care of a small matter for me."

"May I ask you a few questions pertaining to the events?"

"What is it you wish to know?"

"Are the women in your employment usually subjected to violent acts from the gentlemen of the ton?"

Belle released a light laugh. "You make it sound like it is a nightly occurrence. When in fact it rarely happens. The gentlemen who visit my establishment are vetted before I allow them access to any of my girls. They come with the highest references from my regular customers."

"However, one of your girls was violated last night at the hands of a peer."

"You are correct, but I have handled it. The gentleman will no longer be allowed in my club."

"May I also inquire about your club and perhaps speak with a few of your girls?"

"You may ask me questions, but my girls are off limits to anybody who is not a paying customer. I must guard their privacy. It is a promise I have made to them. I won't exploit them any more than what they have chosen."

"How do the girls gain employment?"

"The usual ways—escaping poverty, being disowned by their families, or by tragic life decisions."

"So, aristocratic gentlemen use these less fortunate women for their own selfish pleasures?"

"The pleasures of the flesh are a mutually enjoyed pastime between both sexes. The gentlemen who frequent my establishment seek companionship as well as pleasure. They not only receive pleasure, but they give it as well. All the girls are satisfied upon the completion of a gentleman's visit."

"I don't understand."

"Each gentleman who enters seeks something different from his visit. I pair them with the girl who will fulfill their fantasies. From a man whose only wish is to talk, to a man who desires the taste of a woman. When the gentlemen leave, they are fulfilled from their experience."

"Do the girls ever fall in love?" Phee interjected.

"Yes, my dear, unfortunately some do. When that time comes, I must release them. For it would not end well for the girl or the gentleman."

"That seems cruel to them. Where do they go from here?"

"They are offered a stipend for a simple life."

"What kind of simple life?" asked Phee.

"A life where they follow their own destiny."

"How does this—" A knock interrupted Sidney's question.

Belle rose and opened the door a crack. With a muffled whisper, she gave instructions to the intruder. As she turned, she noticed the two ladies craned their necks for a glimpse of the visitor. One would soon discover the guest, but the other one she would need to occupy while her friend satisfied her curiosity.

"I have decided to let one of you visit with my girls. Would that appease your interests?" Belle directed the question toward Sidney.

Sidney glanced at Phee for approval. She didn't want to abandon her if she objected. She understood Phee's reluctance for this visit and didn't want to subject them to any harm. When Phee nodded her head with enthusiasm, Sid realized Phee was eager to learn how this brothel process worked. With a tilt of her head in agreement, Belle led Sidney to a secret door behind the desk, guiding her into a private room with the promise to return with one of her girls. The madame told Sidney to make herself comfortable as she closed the door between the two rooms. When Sidney turned, she discovered the door held no entryway back into the parlor. With a shrug of her shoulders, she wandered around the room.

While the parlor gave the impression of respectability, this room was meant for pure pleasure. This was how one would expect a brothel to appear. Dark red scarlet walls invited her deeper into the room, with a bed tucked in the corner. Bed hangings decorated in navy blue surrounded the bed. When Sidney peeled the curtains, she discovered a king size mattress covered in silk sheets, with pillows of all sizes scattered near the top. The bed was sin crooking its finger at her, inviting her to lie down and have her every fantasy come to life.

She closed her eyes as her fingers drifted across the smooth bedcover, and her thoughts drifted to Noah Wildeburg. Her overactive imagination conjured images of them tangled between the sheets as they stroked their desires to new heights. His kisses left trails of passion across her body as he aroused her to a need only he could fulfill. Her images brought an ache to her womanly core as her breasts tightened with a need to be touched. She sighed as she lifted a hand to her breasts and brushed across her tight nipples. It was a wonder how her imagination built upon her deepest yearnings.

When Sidney heard the soft click of the door open and close, she lowered her hand and backed away from the bed. She needed to distance herself from the guilty pleasure she indulged in. Embarrassed by her fantasies, a red blush flooded her cheeks as she raised her head to Belle. Only her glance became captured in the stare of her wildest desire, Noah Wildeburg himself.

Chapter Eleven

Wilde leaned against the door as he observed her with lazy indulgence. Nothing went unnoticed from his stare. His fascination took in the dreamy gaze her eyes held to how her nipples tightened through her dress. When Sidney's footsteps brought her toward him, he swiftly closed the gap between them. As he drew her into his embrace, Sidney arched herself closer to him. Their lips hovered over each other as their eyes locked with desire. Sidney's eyes drifted shut as she sighed against his lips. Wilde needed no other encouragement as his mouth devoured what she offered.

When Belle sent him an urgent message, this was not what he expected. He thought she experienced more trouble, and he rushed to her aid. Only when he arrived, Belle informed him of a visitor who required information only he could provide. He thought to ease Belle's troubles but should have been suspicious of her laughter. When he opened the door, he discovered his fantasy in reality.

Wilde didn't care how or why Sidney Hartridge came to be in Belle's house. He only knew of the strong urge to make her his. He watched her as she stroked the bed sheets and saw her expression change to the dreamy quality of sensual desire. When her hand lifted to brush across her breasts, he could no longer deny his need for her.

While he had drank from her lips before, they were kisses meant to tease her into a little playful fun. Fun for him to pass the time until he grew bored. Now her lips tasted of a lust beyond his control. A sweet nectar he wanted to drink from for an eternity. He tilted her head back to draw every last drop of her passion. He nipped and licked, and his tongue stroked hers as she matched his hunger with every stroke of her tongue. Her sighs and moans swallowed in the midst of their long enduring kiss.

After he lifted his head to breathe, he slid his lips to her neck to sample her sweet scent. He inhaled her fragrance, ripe for his taking, as his lips lingered over the beat of her pulse. His tongue trailed to her ear, where he whispered his desire for her. His whispers soon turned to action. He told her about his fantasies as he slowly undid the buttons on her dress. When the dress slid unnoticed between them into a pile on the ground, he raised his head to stare at her in a cotton chemise. While the garment held no sexual appeal, Sidney enticed his need as she stood before him, an erotic version of innocence.

His embrace disheveled her hair, and her eyes were heavily hooded with desire. Her creamy white skin beckoned him to touch her. He trailed his hand across the lace of her chemise, where her breasts were full and invited his touch. She gasped as he slipped his fingers inside to brush across her nipples. When he raised his head to watch her reaction, he found her eyelids fluttering and her teeth biting at her bottom lip. He felt himself harden to a painful reminder of his need for her. He untied her chemise, staring as her breasts spilled into his palms. He stroked his thumbs across the tight pebbles as he continued to watch her.

"When you touched yourself here earlier, I was extremely jealous."

Sidney moaned at his words, her body aching from his sensuous touch. Her need intensified as he caressed her. With each stroke of his tongue and caress of his fingers, her body became enflamed. Only, it wasn't enough. She wanted for more. When he made his presence known, Sidney drifted to him with a desire so strong she would no longer deny herself. The first touch of his lips on hers confirmed her fate to be loved in his arms. His wicked thoughts invaded her mind as he whispered his deepest desires to her. Desires she wished to fulfill with him. Desires her body ached for him to explore. She wanted to be the temptress of his imagination.

"Why?" she moaned as he stroked her nipples. Her dreams held nothing to the actual touch of his fingers.

"I wished for them to be mine."

"Well, they are yours now. What will you do with them?"

"Everything you imagined and then some," he whispered as he lowered his head to draw a bud between his lips.

There were no words to describe the sensations consuming her body. His tongue stroked each nipple into tight buds, drawing them deeper into his mouth to savor. With each pull of his lips on her breasts, she drew in his head in closer for more. While his mouth devoured, his fingers traced underneath and stroked her breasts in his palms. When he finally lifted his head, it was to draw her lips into his, begging her to quench his thirst. She matched the stroke of his tongue, needing the same release he sought. With a swift tug, her chemise now lay atop her dress. She stood before him, naked except for her silk stockings.

She needed to stop this mad desire engulfing them but couldn't. Her scientific mind begged for knowledge, and she held no embarrassment of her own nakedness. She studied the anatomy of men and women and understood the sexual act. The woman inside her pleaded to have her desires fulfilled, and Sidney felt empowered by the admiration of his stare. His eyes portrayed his appreciation of her form, and that knowledge gave her the heady power of her own sexuality. This was no longer about research. This concerned matters of the heart.

Wilde watched as Sidney debated with herself on their course of action. He realized at that moment she understood her power over him. Her midnight eyes grew darker as she reached to undo his cravat. He stood still as she undressed him. Her lips were swollen from biting her lips as she undid the tight buttons of his shirt. When her hands spread his shirt wide and her fingers caressed his chest, he moaned loudly. Her eyes widened, catching him in a stare as she realized the full impact of his desire. However, she was far from finished.

A gleam appeared in her eyes, which only meant trouble for him. Trouble in the form of her hand as it glided across his hardness. When his moan turned into a groan, her eyes lit with satisfaction. Her hand wandered back and laid against his hardness for a moment as he closed his eyes at the immortal pleasure she gifted him. Sidney's pleasant torture had only just begun. Her hand stroked him outside his trousers, and his pleasure grew firmer from her touch. He finally laid his hand across hers to halt her contact. If she were to continue, he could no longer fulfill their greatest need.

He raised her hand to his lips while he kissed the fingers that caressed him into his frenzy desired state. His kisses lowered themselves again to her breasts and slid across her stomach as he knelt before her. His fingers drifted across her soft curls as he lowered her stockings. After her legs were bare, he stroked his fingers along the back of her knees and around to her thighs. He placed soft kisses to her legs until they parted for him. Softly he slid his finger across her core, her wetness coating the tip. He closed his eyes and moaned at her need. Slowly he guided his finger inside her, her warmth drawing him in deeper. His finger reached higher as he stroked her wetness. In and out his finger glided as he built her ache for him. He wanted her to crave him as badly as he ached. He wanted her need to be as soul deep as his was for her. When she tightened around his finger, he pulled out and rested his head against her core. He could feel her body tightly strung and heard the hitch in her breath as he brought her close to fulfillment. He placed a gentle kiss against her need.

"Next time, I will bring you to a fevered need with my mouth. I will stroke your desires with my tongue as I savor your wetness," he whispered as he slid his fingers inside her again.

Sidney wanted to cry from the emotions crashing around inside her body. Her imagination gained new heights from those whispered words. She arched her body into his mouth, wanting him to show her now. Instead, he rose and took her mouth in his to assault her senses. Each kiss slowly dragged her under his spell. When he grabbed her hand, he lowered it to his hardness. While he kissed her, he managed to undo the placket of his trousers and kick them off into the pile of their discarded clothing. He wrapped her hand around his and guided her on how to stroke his desire. He whispered in her ear how her touch drove him mad and that he wished for her lips to follow her hand.

Soon Wilde lifted Sidney into his arms and lay her amongst the silken sheets and pillows. He could wait no longer. Wilde needed her with a power out of his control. His hands slid to her thighs, where she opened for him in anticipation. Her eagerness became his undoing. He slid his hardness along her wetness as he guided himself inside her. When she lifted her hips to him, her fingers dug into his back, and he hesitated, not wishing to harm her. When she wrapped her legs around his hips and drove him deeper, he couldn't stop. Her desire matched his as they dove into their passion. With each stroke, she wrapped her body around him to hold him closer. When he slowly pulled out and swiftly entered her again, she moaned for more. Their need, consumed by every touch and kiss, melted their bodies into one. When her wetness tightened around him, he released himself into her, drowning in her kiss.

Wilde drew her close to his heart and stroked her hair across his chest as their hearts slowed down. They were too lost in their passion to realize the depth of her ruination. He wanted to question her on her visit to Belle's but didn't want to break the spell. Their time was limited, but Belle would soon interrupt them. He needed Sidney to leave without getting caught. The hour grew late, and soon the house would fill with their fellow peers. He rolled her over and brushed the hair from her eyes. She met his gaze, eyes filled with an emotion he didn't want her to feel.

"Why did you come here?"

"Curiosity on what draws your attention."

"It is not this place."

"Are you sure? You appear quite comfortable in these surroundings. Also, I heard of your good deed last night."

"You shouldn't have been privy to that information. It is too vulgar for one of your station."

"Nonsense. It showed me that underneath your scoundrel charm, there resides a man of true character. You display a set of traits more pleasing than another suiter of mine."

"Sheffield is a selfish bastard."

"Mmm, I quite agree with you. However, he holds promises in other matters."

"What might those matters be?" Wilde growled.

Sidney laughed. "You will soon discover."

"Sidney?"

"So, did I fulfill your every fantasy? Madame Belle informed me of a gentleman's wishes when he frequents her establishment." Sidney ignored his question.

"You misunderstand my relationship with Belle."

"How so? Have you visited this room before?"

"Yes, but only as a friend. I have never partaken in a sexual relationship with Belle."

"But you have shared sexual encounters with the women she employs?"

"Yes, but—"

"Then I misunderstand nothing."

"I have not used those services since the night I met you." Wilde became agitated at her nonchalant attitude toward their lovemaking, as if it were an experiment of sort.

"So, the evening we met was your last attempt of a sexual release?"

"Yes. No."

"Which is it? Yes or No?"

Wilde breathed a rush of air in his frustration at the turn of their conversation. She mixed his words around.

"After the Woodsworth Ball, I visited Belle's. While sampling one of her girl's charms, I kept picturing you, and I couldn't stop thinking of your lips, so I left. To answer your question, yes, I came, but no, I didn't finish."

Sidney stilled at this knowledge. Did she hold an impact on Wildeburg's affections? Did his love flourish as hers did? He mentioned nothing concerning his emotions or a relationship after they made love. Was she another scandal for him? Would he disappear now that he finished the chase? Too many questions to wonder, and fear kept her from discovering the answers. While his lovemaking satisfied her curiosity, it also opened Wilde to cause her more heartache.

"I didn't finish because you had consumed my mind. The touch of your lips, the midnight blue of your eyes darkening at my touch, and the sighs you whisper when I am near. So, as to your question, have you fulfilled my fantasy? Yes, although in this short time, I have only created more."

Wilde slid his mouth across her cheek, his tongue burning a trail of fire down her neck as his hands caressed her breasts. Her silence unnerved him. He figured if he kept their desire burning, she would hold no doubts in her mind. When he heard her sigh, he knew he distracted her from her thoughts. As his mouth followed his hands to her breasts, a knock on the door interrupted them. He rested his head on her chest as he brought himself under control. Their time had come to an end.

With a whispered word, he wrapped a sheet around his body and opened the door a crack. Belle waited on the other side with a disapproving frown upon her face. Their whispered argument discussed her displeasure. While Belle worked in the profession of sex, she believed in a young lady's honor. His actions would have huge repercussions for her. He promised Belle he would prepare Sidney for a discreet departure. He closed the door and leaned against the panel, closing his eyes as he realized the full consequences of his heated desires. As he glanced to the bed, Sidney regarded him with questions in her eyes. He couldn't answer the unspoken when he himself was just as confused.

"Our time has come to part. The hour grows late, and you are sure to be missed. Belle has a carriage awaiting your departure."

"Wilde?"

"Hurry, Lady Sophia and you must return home before you are ruined."

"Am I not already ruined?"

"You know full well what I am implying."

"Mmm, yes I suppose I do." Sidney rose from the bed to put herself back together.

As she dressed, she blocked her emotions from Wilde. His indifference toward her shattered her frame of mind. One moment he began to make love to her again, the next he ordered her to leave. All while offering no promises. She peeked beneath her lashes as she slid on her stockings, watching him pace back and forth across the room. He appeared agitated. Did he regret their lovemaking and wondered how to dissociate himself from her?

"I am ready, but you can inform Belle her carriage will not be necessary. My coach is in the alleyway. Please inform my driver we are ready to leave," Sidney told Wilde as she brushed the wrinkles from her skirts.

Wilde strode to the door and informed Belle of Sidney's request. His guilt weighed heavily on his mind. He realized he hurt her with his rush for her to leave. He either had to send her on her way, or he would lock the door and make love to her all night. Her ruination be damned. He slowly walked to her and stood mere inches from her. Their gazes clashed, and each asked questions from the other. When neither of them answered, they took a step closer.

"As always, your charm has been most enlightening, Lord Wildeburg."

"Noah."

When she didn't call him Noah, he brought her flush against his body. The questions disappeared from her eyes as desire darkened them. He swept his lips across hers, teasing them with small kisses. He wanted her to whisper his name from the very lips he kissed. When she still didn't utter his one simple name, he took her mouth under his and kissed her passionately. He ravaged her mouth with his pent-up passion. Each stroke of his tongue demanded her need in return.

Sidney held nothing back from their kiss. With each kiss of his lips to the stroke of his tongue, she responded with her desire. His actions confused her. He switched hot, then cold, then hot again. Sidney, lost in her own emotions, ceased to pay attention. She only responded to what she felt, and her body spun out of control. Her need for him consumed her. As quickly as he kissed her, he also pulled away. She didn't want the kiss to end. She wanted to taste more of him.

"Noah," she moaned.

A bittersweet laugh escaped him as he listened to his name on her lips. As he rested his forehead against hers, he struggled to breathe again. With another knock on the door, he knew she needed to return home. Timing was not on his side. There was much he needed to discuss with her, but now wasn't the time nor the place. He brushed his lips across hers for one final kiss before he stepped away.

"Noah?"

"You must leave. Belle is waiting for you."

"Will I see you soon?" Sidney begged for his attention.

"We shall see."

Sidney narrowed her eyes at his cryptic answer. Frustrated with his hot and cold attitude, she strode out of the room and found Belle wearing a concerned expression on her face. The woman glanced behind her to find

Wildeburg with a devil may care attitude and a smile of smug satisfaction. Sidney turned at the same moment to witness their exchange and tears rushed to her eyes. She finally realized that she was only another notch in his bedpost. Belle wrapped her arms around her and guided Sidney toward the back door, where her carriage waited to take her home.

"I am sorry, My Lady. If I had known, I would never have called for him."

"You are not at fault, Madame. I am a woman who makes my own decisions. As I told him, he was most enlightening, as usual. Thank you for granting me your time today."

Belle nodded her head as Sidney's footman helped her into the carriage. Sophia sat tucked in the corner, lost in her own thoughts. As the carriage drove them home, neither lady discussed the events they experienced at Madame Bellerose's brothel. Each activity, if known, would lead them to a ruination that their fathers' statuses in the ton could not sweep under the rug.

Chapter Twelve

The next few days passed in a blur for Sidney. Her confused emotions conflicted with her research, and she lost interest in writing her thesis. She only needed the results from the upcoming ball to apply her final touches to the paper. However, her heart no longer cared about the results. She had not heard from Noah since their encounter at Madame Bellerose's. No gifts, no midnight invasions into her bedroom, and no surprise visits at the park. Only his absence, which only made her think she was correct in her assumptions about his behavior. He was a charming scoundrel who played her false, just so he could whet his appetite. His part of her research helped support her claims. She wrote passionately on his section, for every word held her deepest emotions.

Sidney wrote about Rory on how she predicted the outcome. She discussed his awareness of her as a woman but pointed toward his strengths. Their friendship held more importance than a mere misguided attraction. Rory showed his compassion toward her this week as he tagged along on her walks, without a single word being spoken. He was there for her in ways that mattered. He took notice of her sadness and offered his friendship. Sidney suffered through her guilt at deceiving him and using his friendship to prove a theory. She would offer her apologies when she concluded her experiment. For now, she took solace in their relationship.

Sophia had been absent, which was probably why she had been leaning on Rory more. Sophia returned her missives, pleading outings with her mother as excuses. Sidney wondered at her claims but was too wrapped in her own sorrow to question them. Phee sent a note, promising to help her prepare for the Havelock Ball. All in all, Sidney behaved as a horrible friend this week and realized she needed to make amends to those close to her after the ball was over.

Sidney wandered downstairs to her father's study. She decided to immerse herself in his research to keep her mind off her own troubles. As she entered the room, she found her father in a deep conversation with Sheffield—the other suitor who was absent this week. When they noticed her, their conversation came to a halt. Her father's eyes held disappointment in his stare, while Sheffield's held victory. She realized they were discussing her. What information had Sheffield shared with her father that caused him to regard her in shame?

"I will leave you two for a private moment. I thank you for your honorable intentions, Your Grace. You do my family a favor, and we will be forever in your debt. Sidney, please join me in the garden when you finish your talk with Sheffield."

"Yes, Papa."

The weight of apprehension settled on Sidney's shoulders. She had upset her father in a way she never had before. What story did Sheffield weave to him? Why did she feel doomed to a life that wasn't her choosing? When her stare settled on Sheffield, she recognized that her selfish actions from a few days ago caused Sheffield to claim her as his bride. Did Wildeburg brag of his conquest to her ruination? Was he here to wipe away his friend's mistake?

Sidney settled in a chair and folded her hands in her lap. She held her head high, with her chin raised in defiance. She wouldn't allow this man, or any other man, to determine the course of her life. Even though Noah—no, Lord Wildeburg—discarded her after their exquisite lovemaking, she wouldn't regret their time together. He taught her of passion and heartache, two emotions that helped her understand her own vulnerability about love.

Sheffield watched as Sidney Hartridge realized her own demise. While he should feel complete satisfaction in his victory, there was a part of him infuriated beyond belief. He had only won her hand out of the misguided antics of his friend, a friend who had disappeared this past week. When he finally located Wilde, he discovered him in a drunken stupor. Wilde rambled on how he took advantage of Lady Sidney and was unworthy of her. When he confided how much he loved her, and the details of her ruination, Sheffield realized the game swung his way. If he could approach her father before Wildeburg, then her hand would be his. He waited the last week for his friend to approach Lord Hartridge, but when Wilde didn't appear, Sheffield moved in to claim his victory.

Sheffield already knew of Sidney Hartridge's downfall. He was at Belle's when she appeared from Belle's private chambers, her appearance in dishevel. Her hair hung unwound along her back, and her clothes were wrinkled beyond repair. The fullness of her lips portrayed a woman who had been kissed quite thoroughly. As Belle ushered Sidney to her carriage, he stood in the alcove and watched as Wildeburg sauntered out of the chamber. He strutted with the swagger of a man well satisfied. He kept his appearance hidden as Wilde left the brothel. When Belle reappeared, he questioned her, for her to spell out the mistake she made this afternoon. She called Wildeburg to her house after Lady Sidney arrived and mentioned his name.

She hoped Wilde would remove the girl, but instead he made love to her, an action which could destroy her brothel if nobody offered for the girl's hand. Sheffield promised her he would make right by Sidney Hartridge. It was the least he could do since he didn't help her the previous evening. If he could secure Lady Sidney as a bride, then he could frequent Belle's again, to catch a few more moments with the mystery woman he met.

"You wish a word with me, Your Grace."

"I have spoken to your father, and we have reached an agreement."

"On?"

"I have agreed to offer for your hand in marriage, in exchange for your family to escape the scandal you have brought to their lives."

"What scandal might that be?"

"You were seen leaving a brothel in the middle of the afternoon."

"What rubbish. Who spreads such lies?"

"Are they lies, Lady Sidney? Do you require proof of your disgrace?"

Sidney narrowed her eyes. She didn't trust Sheffield and thought he bluffed. Is this how Wilde ended his affairs?

"Yes, actually, I do."

"You wore one of your dowdy day dresses, which was wrinkled beyond repair. Your hair was unbound and tousled down your back. It was your lips that gave you away the most. They were full, pouty, and appeared quite ravished. As you left Madame Bellerose's private chambers, Lord Wildeburg soon followed you. Does any of this information provide you with proof?"

Sidney stilled. He had described her appearance to a tee. For him to give that detailed of a description meant he witnessed her mistake. With this knowledge, he gained the upper hand and went to any length to secure her as his bride. By her father's disappointment, she knew Sheffield had told him. It seemed she would be his duchess after all. He made no mention of Sophia's whereabouts at the brothel. Did he keep the information as bait to blackmail her later if she refused? She couldn't allow Sophia's reputation to be tarnished too. If not for her, Sophia would never have joined her at Madame Bellerose's establishment. She would do anything to protect her friend.

"Does Papa know?"

"Only of your appearance at the brothel, not of your association with Wildeburg."

"Did Lord Wildeburg send you to clean up his mistake, or do you make offers for all of your friends' discarded lovers to make them your bride?"

"No, Wildeburg is unaware of my intentions. He is otherwise occupied with his own agenda to concern himself over my affairs."

"Why then?

"Why not? I have courted you this season for this very reason. When an opportunity lands in my lap, I make a success of it. I sense we will have an engaging marriage. I have deemed you to be my duchess, so you will be. No other offers will come your way."

Sheffield watched the hurt enter her eyes as he let his threat hang in the air. He downplayed Wilde to cause doubt in her mind. If she thought Wilde moved on to his next conquest, then it would secure him her hand. Sheffield knew his time was precious. Soon, Wilde would come to his senses and propose to the chit. Before that happened, he needed to move fast to bring her to the altar. After he announced their engagement, she would not dare rescind. Nor would her parents allow it. As he continued his stare, he saw the moment she admitted defeat to her situation.

"Very well. I accept your offer of marriage. I only ask that you do not share my full shame with my parents."

"Agreed. I see no need to hurt my new in-laws. I respect your father too much."

"Thank you, Your Grace."

"I see no reason why you should not call me Alexander. Alex, if you wish."

"Alex."

"We shall announce our betrothal at the Havelock Ball tomorrow evening."

"If you insist."

"I do, Sidney. As soon as we can establish your devotion, then no gossip will spread about your attachment with Wildeburg. I have always considered him to be a close friend, but I will have to separate my association with him, I think. I cannot have my reputation ruined by rumors of my duchess cuckolding me with my best friend."

Sidney sat up straighter. "I would never dishonor you in that regard, Your Grace."

Sheffield laughed. "You are not the one I worry about, my dear."

Sheffield rose and strolled to Sidney, offering his hand to help her rise. He raised her hand to his lips, where he turned her hand over and placed a kiss inside her palm. He then lowered his head to brush a kiss across her cheek. As his lips drifted to her lips, Sidney turned her head to the side. His kiss landed on the side of her head as she stepped away from him. He took pleasure at her discomfort. It would be to his advantage later.

"I will make all the arrangements. Please inform your parents of my arrival tomorrow at eight o'clock to escort your family to the ball."

With those parting words, he staked his claim on her. Sidney sighed as she glanced around Papa's study. She dreaded meeting him in the garden. His disapproval hurt. She hoped her engagement to Sheffield would ease his anger. As she slowly walked to the garden, she saw Papa sitting on the bench against the back fence. Her fingers trailed over the bench that reminded her so much of Noah as she continued to her father's side. Those memories would be no more. She needed to tuck them away in her heart. Her father patted his side as he smiled sadly at her. She settled against his side and laid her head on his shoulder.

"I'm sorry, Papa," she whispered.

"You have accepted his proposal."

"Yes, I never meant to cause scandal on our family with my actions."

"Ah, Sidney you are your father's daughter. Like me, you act before you think. We are scientists, my dear, and think there are probable reasons for every course of action."

"Yes, but my action caused harm."

"Nonsense. Sheffield stopped you from suffering any shame. We will be indebted to his sacrifice."

Sidney didn't reply. This was a position she never wanted for herself or her family. Sheffield and her parents were unaware of the false promise she gave the duke. She had no intention of walking down the aisle with Sheffield. She only needed to publish her story for the truth to come out. Oh, she knew Sheffield held knowledge of her affair with Wildeburg, but when she exposed Sheffield as the conceited ass he was, he would end the engagement out of embarrassment. He would not wed a lady who exposed his faults to the entire ton. After she finished with him, no lady would favor his courtship. Sophia had been right about the duke.

"He will arrive at eight o'clock to accompany us to the ball tomorrow."

"I will inform your mama of your betrothal. I do not want her to hear the true reason why the duke offered for your hand. She will believe he fell in love with you and cannot wait for your marriage. He told me he will make arrangements for you to wed soon."

"Yes, Papa," Sidney agreed.

"As to your visit to the brothel, I'm sure you are aware of your bad decision and will not make the same mistake again. As for the reason, did you gain the information you needed for your research, or do you need me to answer some questions for you?"

Sidney pulled away and stared at her father in disbelief. "You know about my research. How?"

"I don't know the specifics of your project. Sidney, you have helped me since you were ten years old. Your curiosity has always gotten the better of you. I assume your research has something to do with your foray into the season and the attendance of the young chaps who have invaded my house on a daily basis. So, have you proved your theory yet?"

"Tomorrow night at the ball will help me finish my thesis."

"Do you think that is wise, Sidney?"

"I promise not to cause a scandal, Papa. I only wish to prove my theory. Then I will write and publish my findings."

"Sidney, you cannot publish your work anymore. It is not the proper behavior of a duchess."

"Don't worry, Papa, I will write under an alias."

Lord Hartridge sighed. "All right. Now I am off to tell Mama the wonderful news of your betrothal. So, beware, she will bombard you with visits to the shops. I will keep her as occupied as I can today, but after the

Havelock Ball, the entire ton will know of your engagement to the duke. I expect you to keep your mother happy during this time; her greatest dream for you has come true."

Sidney rose with her father and followed him into the house. She decided to join him as he told Mama her news. Her father meant to protect her from her mother's enthusiasm, but since she caused the debacle, she would tolerate her mother's joy for the time being. She cringed to herself on how short-lived her mother's delight would be.

~~~~~~

Wilde stood amongst the trees in the back alley, hidden from the occupants in the garden. He listened as Sidney discussed her engagement with her father. Duchess? Damn, Sheffield continued the game. He should have known better when his friend appeared concerned for him yesterday. Sheffield already planned his own hidden agenda. He struck while Wilde was down.

His own consumption of multiple bottles of whiskey still didn't wane his desire for Sidney Hartridge. In his drunken stupor, he realized his reasons for drinking. He wished to escape the affairs of his heart. She ensnared his heart and held it captive, and his love for her consumed him. Since he had never experienced this feeling, he was unprepared on how to deal with the emotions. After he sobered, he realized he needed to ask for her hand in marriage. He thought she might have suffered heartache from his disappearance in her life. Fool that he was, she already secured herself a groom.

He lurked in his hiding place as he listened to their conversation. Her words were soft and muffled, but they held the sweet melody he enjoyed. He became lost in their voices until her father objected to a paper she wrote. Wilde listened more closely to the details and learned Sidney conducted a research project on her suitors. That was why she entered the marriage mart for the season. He laughed to himself as he realized she played her own game against them. They were no match for her. She didn't elaborate on the details, but Wilde understood the subjects of her research. Every single gentleman of the ton, including himself.

After Sidney and her father left the garden, Wilde stepped out of his shelter. He stood at the back of the gate as he watched them walk inside the house. A plan formed in his mind to win her back. Sheffield would not be the victor. He walked away, whistling an offbeat tune, his mood greatly improved. Sidney Hartridge would not be a duchess, but a marchioness instead.

Chapter Thirteen

The ball started the same as the first ball of the season. Sidney stood on the outskirts, surveying the ballroom floor while her friend Sophia stood nervously at her side. Only this time, Phee didn't try to convince her of what a horrible idea her research was. If anything, her friend remained subdued. She arrived early to help Sidney prepare for the ball. When Sidney informed Phee of her recent engagement to the duke, she expected Phee to be angry at Sheffield for cornering her. She thought Phee would rant and rave her displeasure. Instead, Phee remained silent after the initial shock.

Sidney noticed two of her subjects enter the ballroom. Lord Rory Beckwith walked to her parents' side and engaged her father in a discussion. Lord Noah Wildeburg sauntered into the ballroom, with every female following his path. The widows and married ladies of the ton tried to grab his attention as he passed them by. However, they were unlucky to draw his interest. Instead, he wandered to the wallflower corner and enticed a young lady into a dance. Sidney craned her neck as she tried to catch a glimpse of the couple. All she could make out was the fiery shade of her red hair coupled with the most obnoxious color of her dress—a dark shade of pink that washed out her complexion. Each time their steps drew nearer, Wilde swept the young miss away across the room. Obviously, the marquess had found himself his next conquest. The sudden ache in her chest made Sidney want to double over in pain. As she stared at him holding another in his arms, it became too much for her to bear.

"Who is she?" Sidney whispered to herself.

"Lady Dallis MacPherson. She hails from Inverness and has come to visit her grandmother for the season," Sophia replied.

"Who is her grandmother?"

"Lady Ratcliff."

Sidney grimaced. "Poor thing. She doesn't have a chance."

"It would appear her luck will change after her dance with Lord Wildeburg."

"You mean her reputation will be torn to shreds."

"No, I mean, since Wildeburg asked for her hand in a dance, he has secured her a successful season. Every man will compete for her to fight against Wildeburg's chances," Phee refuted.

"That is sad then, for the gentlemen will not behold what Lady Dallis truly has to offer."

"I think the right gentleman will. Not everybody is as jaded as you are, Sidney. I think your research on this project has clouded your mind. No, more like your heart. I warned you of this, and now you are cynical by this stupid notion that gentlemen only have one goal in mind when they pursue a lady. I am saddened by your inability to open your heart to love."

"There is much I haven't told you, Phee. I opened my heart, only to have Wildeburg slam it shut again. Now, I am engaged to marry a man I do not love and do not want to wed. After I have finished my paper, we need to have a long talk. I realize something bothers you, and with my own struggles, I have neglected our friendship. Please be patient with me, and I promise to make amends. Tomorrow we will have an afternoon of hot chocolate and biscuits, and you can read to me from one of your romantic novels."

Sophia reached over to embrace Sidney. When she pulled away, she linked her pinkie with Sidney's. Only she couldn't tell Sidney what troubled her, for it involved Sidney's betrothed. No, her secret would have to stay hidden in her own heart. She wouldn't hurt her friend with what transpired between her and Sheffield. She would have to develop a story to pacify Sidney. As Sidney linked her finger with hers and made a joke, Sophia glanced over her shoulder to notice the Duke of Sheffield entering the ballroom. Sidney explained how Sheffield escorted them to the ball, then a group of his friends drew him away to the card room. His return sent Sophia's heart racing.

Sidney noticed the rapid change in Sophia's demeanor. Her face paled and her eyes grew large when she glanced over Sidney's shoulder. Phee dropped Sidney's hand and nervously smoothed her palms along her skirts, then pretended interest with the contents inside her reticule. Sidney looked over her shoulder to watch as Sheffield walked over to them. She then glanced between the two. Sheffield appeared indifferent to her friend, but Sophia's cheeks blushed a bright shade of red. When Sheffield greeted them, Sophia stuttered a response.

"Oh, look, Mama is waving me her way. I will see you at dinner, Sidney, Your Grace." Sophia made her excuses, leaving them alone.

"Your friend is an odd duck."

"She is not. Sophia is my dearest friend in the world."

"Who is Wildeburg's dance partner?" Sheffield asked. He already forgot about Lady Sophia as he drew Sidney's attention to Wildeburg's newest mark.

"She is Lady Dallis, the granddaughter of Lady Ratcliff."

Sheffield winced. "Poor girl."

"Yes, my sentiments exactly." Sidney stared as Wilde escorted Lady Dallis to her grandmother.

Soon the dance floor cleared, and Lady Havelock asked for her guests' attention. She announced her excitement about the Duke of Sheffield's engagement at her ball. Heads whipped in her direction. The crowded ballroom began to whisper and search for the duke.

"I believe that is our cue, my dear." Sheffield ushered Sidney to the hostess.

Sidney's parents joined them near the musicians as Sheffield boasted his engagement to the ton. He made a romantic speech regarding their courtship, which had the guests laughing alongside him. Then her father gave a speech, welcoming the duke into their family. She could not recall what they spoke because Noah captured her attention with his stare. His eyes held a hurt only she related to. However, his gaze quickly turned to anger. Sheffield pulled her close to his side and slid a ring onto her finger. With a tilt of his head and a twist to his lips, Noah bowed in her direction before he turned and walked away. Before long, well-wishers surrounded them. The gentlemen patted him on the back, declaring him a lucky man, while the ladies masked their good wishes with snide remarks covered in sweet words. Their glances in her direction spoke otherwise.

Soon the guests pushed her to the side as they plied Sheffield with compliments, with the hope of an invitation to the wedding. As she stood, forgotten, somebody gripped her arm and swept her near the balcony doors. As they preceded outdoors, Sidney took a look at her rescuer. Rory frowned as he dragged her down the stairs and into the garden. His face held the evidence of his frustration. Sidney knew if she didn't calm him soon, his temper would explode. She laid her hand on his arm and brought him to a stop. He pulled away from her and stalked down the path and back to her again.

"Are you going to explain why you are engaged to that pompous jackass?"

Sidney sighed. "He caught me in a compromising position and informed Papa. They reached an agreement to make me his duchess."

"What sort of compromising position?"

"The sort that involves a brothel and a scoundrel of the ton."

"Wildeburg."

"Yes."

"Damn, Sidney. I warned you of these men."

"I know." She sighed again as she settled on the bench nearby.

"Then, why did you proceed with this madness?"

Sidney decided to confide in Rory about her experiment. "I'm researching how a gentleman will ruin a lady for his own pleasure. I wanted to draw three subjects into an attempt to kiss me in a private setting and note how they would protect my honor."

"Was I one of your subjects?"

She winced when she looked him in the eye. "Yes."

"I'm assuming the other two subjects were Sheffield and Wildeburg."

"Yes."

"I will even go one step further and assume Wildeburg was the scoundrel who seduced you, and Sheffield is blackmailing you into a marriage you want no part of. Am I correct again?"

"You are."

"Well, there seems to be only one solution to part of this mess."

"And that is?"

Rory slid next to Sidney on the bench and pulled her into his arms. "Simple, I shall give you one of those kisses you require for your project. This will cause a scandal, and Sheffield will withdraw his offer." He lowered his head to place a kiss upon her lips.

Before his lips met hers, somebody yanked Rory away. A pair of arms swung him around and planted a fist on his cheek. Soon, punches flew from both gentlemen. Some connected with grunts echoing their pain. Sidney watched in horror as Noah and Rory pounded each other, neither of them holding back their anger. Soon Sheffield forced them apart by shoving himself in between the two with his arms held out. Sidney's hand became clasped in comfort as Sophia joined her in the mix. Sophia glared at the gentlemen—Sheffield in particular.

"Let go of me, Sheffield. After I am done with him, you are next," Rory growled.

"Stand in line, Beckwith. Sheffield is mine," Wildeburg gritted between his teeth.

"Now, gentlemen, why are you angry with me? Especially tonight of all occasions, we should be sharing a toast as we smoke cigars while you congratulate me on my good fortune."

"Good fortune? You have underhandedly taken from me what is mine," replied Wilde.

"Well my good friend, you waited too long. I am the victor to this game. You played it well. I thought I had lost, but when you hesitated on your last move, I claimed the prize."

"Game? Prize?" Sidney questioned.

"You were nothing but a game to these scoundrels. Each man set out to see who could win your hand, no rules allowed," Rory explained.

"Was that all I ever was to you?" Sidney confronted Noah with tears in her eyes. Her voice caught as she watched the guilt spread across his face.

"Let me—"

Sidney held her hand to stop him. "I am nobody's prize. You, sir, are a shallow cad." She then turned toward Sheffield. "You, sir, are a manipulative swine." She finally settled on Rory. "And I thought you were my friend." Sidney ran from the garden but halted when Wilde spoke.

"We were not the only ones playing a game though, were we Lady Sidney?"

Sidney slowly swung toward the group of men. "Excuse me?"

"You, yourself, played a game against us." Noah spread his arms out wide indicating Rory, Sheffield, and himself.

Sidney swung her eyes to Rory and Phee, who both shook their heads in denial. When she looked to Sheffield, it was to see his eyes narrow and a scowl spread across his face. She sensed his anger as he realized she had made a fool of him. If the names she called him didn't break their betrothal, then the truth of her deception would. She didn't know how Wilde discovered her secret, but it wouldn't stop her from finishing what she started. She pulled her shoulders back and stood before them, proud of herself and her determination to uncover the depth of a man's deception.

"You are quite correct, Lord Wildeburg. A few weeks ago, I devised a research project set to expose the scandalous ways of the gentlemen of the ton. I chose three subjects to write my thesis on. The theory was to prove how three separate men would lure me into a private setting to steal a kiss or other favors. Then I wanted to prove how they would risk my reputation and the lengths they would go to secure my ruination."

Sidney paused, waiting for a reaction. When none came, she continued. "I chose one from each rank of the peerage by their reputation. I desired to receive a kiss from each of you. First a duke. Sheffield, I wanted to see if, after you kissed me, you would then offer for my hand. I speculated on how far somebody as high ranking as a duke would go to seduce an innocent.

"The second gentlemen was a marquess. Wildeburg, I heard tales of your disgraceful nature. How you ruined young misses. The data I collected on you proved to be correct on how I assumed you would handle your affairs.

"The third, an earl. Beckwith, my decision to choose a friend came from the question of your reaction to the change in my appearance. I wondered if you would alter your behavior toward me.

"I inserted many variables into my research to be proven wrong. But alas, I was not. Each of you gentlemen have confirmed my theory. I thank you for your assistance in helping me to conclude my research."

With her speech delivered with no interruptions, Sidney turned on her heel and departed the garden for the ballroom. She wished to find her parents and leave all this behind her. She felt guilty for leaving Sophia but knew Rory would escort her back to her parents. Once her deception settled into Sheffield's mind, he would ruin her family. If she managed to put some distance between them, they could at least avoid a scandal at the ball. Her parents stood on the balcony, waiting for her. Her mother was quite upset, and her father wore a frown. Sidney realized they witnessed her speech and were appalled. Sidney felt an arm circle her waist and heard Rory tell her father that his carriage would take them home. He helped her father usher her mother to the front of the Havelocks' home.

"Rory. You left Phee alone, I have to—"

"Go with your parents. I will see to Sophia."

Sidney squeezed his hand in gratitude. "I am sorry for betraying our friendship with false airs."

"It better be one hell of a paper, Sid."

Sidney's laugh was bitter. "It will be."

Soon they settled in Rory's carriage and headed home. Her mother shed tears and moaned her embarrassment, threatening to send her to a convent. While her father shook his head and added his disappointment about her theatrics in the garden. He even agreed with Mama's comments on the convent, since he fully understood her ruination. Once they arrived home, her parents ordered her to her bedroom for the duration of the evening. Her father informed her they would discuss her future in the morning when tensions weren't so high.

As Sidney trudged her way up the stairs to her bedroom, she understood the full impact of her destruction. She selfishly ruined the respect of her parents' standing in the ton, not to mention her relationship with them. They would no longer trust her actions, and she didn't blame them. She had not only hurt her parents, but she had also hurt her friends as well. In her self-absorption, she neglected her friendship with Phee. Something troubled her, but Sidney didn't set aside her own needs for those of Phee's. Her relationship with Rory would be strained now too. She caused doubt in his mind with her deception, playing on her appearance to fool him. However, as much as she was at fault, it would not sway her decision to write her paper. The truth needed to be spread, and she would—in detail.

Chapter Fourteen

When she wandered into her room, her window stood open. The cool breeze swept inside, blowing the curtains in the air. Sidney twirled around, expecting Noah to be waiting for her. But alas, the room stood empty. She hurried to the windows to glimpse outside, but he was nowhere to be seen.

"I am sorry, My Lady. In my clumsiness, I tipped over a bottle of your perfume, and the air was heavy. I opened the room to clear away the odor. Allow me to close the windows for you." Rose latched the windows, then turned to help Sidney undress.

Sidney stood still, disappointed as Rose removed her dress and helped her into a nightgown and robe. Rose wanted to gossip about Sidney's engagement, but she pleaded tiredness and sent Rose on her way after she brushed out Sidney's hair. Sidney tugged back the covers and climbed into bed. When she reached over to blow out her lantern, she saw her book lying on the side table. Sidney laughed at the irony of the book. She decided to read a few pages, hoping they would help her fall asleep. What better way to finish the evening than to read about the one subject she botched. Romance. There would be no more romance in her future. From what she experienced this season, she was unsure if she ever wanted to again.

As her fingers drifted through the novel to find her spot, an envelope floated out from between the pages. A parchment of paper folded with a seal and addressed with her name on the outside rested on the blanket. Curious as to how a letter to her became hidden inside her book, she broke the seal to see who wrote to her.

My darling Sidney,

I find I have many reasons to apologize to you. First reason would be for stealing your book and not returning it to you. I've had your book in my possession since the first meeting in our park. My reference to Hillside Park as ours is because it is the spot where you invaded my heart. I kept your book to help me find a way to steal your heart. During my pursuit, I read the novel and incorporated the hero's actions into my own. I also confess to charming your dear friend Sophia to assist me with your gifts.

Please don't be angry with her for helping me woo you. She is a wonderful friend, and I do not want to be the reason for any rift between you two. When I told her of my plans, she only wished to help with your happiness. Which I have seemed to blunder.

Second, I apologize for exposing your research secret. I overheard your conversation with your father when you discussed the matter. While I was not angry, but impressed with how your mind works, I was jealous of your betrothal to Sheffield. I wanted to sabotage your engagement and realized this was my move for revenge.

Third, I am very sorry if I have ruined your engagement. I never meant to cause your family a scandal. I set you up to be taken advantage of by Sheffield with my lateness in asking for your hand. I do take back part of my apology. For I am not sorry if Sheffield has withdrawn his promise to make you his duchess.

Fourth, I was a fool to play a game with Sheffield to win your affections. Everything has always been a game between us. Women, cards, drinking, you name it and we would compete. You were supposed to be no different, just a chit we could toy with for the season. However, Sheffield changed the stakes when he talked of marriage. I would not allow him to win your hand.

The final reason in my apology is for leaving you to wonder of my regards. The feelings you invoked in me frightened me. Terrified actually. In concern of my own fears, I left you in doubt of my intentions.

The most memorable experience of my life was making love to you. There are no words to describe how you touched my soul. I am ashamed of myself in how I took advantage of you and where. Part of the shame has kept me from your side. I tried to convince myself any man would be better for you than me, even Sheffield. But as I came to my senses, I realized I was wrong. I aspire to be the man you deserve. For the rest of our lives together I want to prove my love to you.

There are many apologies I must make to you and your family, and starting tomorrow I shall begin. Can you find it in your heart to forgive me? I understand if you do not love me, but I will spend the rest of my life trying to earn your love and respect. I wanted to remain in your room to watch your reaction but realized I could no longer ruin your reputation. Below your window, I await in the garden for your reaction. If you would grant me my wish and at least come to the window, I will know I stand a chance to win your heart. If not, I understand, but it will not deter me to win your affections, for I have many tricks up my sleeve to prove my love for you.

I am truly sorry, my dear.

I love you deeply with all my heart.

Your most shameful suitor,

Noah

Sidney let the letter slide to her lap as she let his words impact her decision. Should she rise from the bed and check the garden, or should she stay beneath the covers? He tempted her to see if he waited below, but the rational part of her brain debated the sincerity of his letter. It appeared their whole affair was nothing but a bunch of lies on both of their parts. Could they ever trust one another to not deceive? While Sidney's heart shouted yes, the rest of her remained confused. The confused side of her mind kept her under the blanket. She stared at the windows, wishing she could see the garden from the bed. Sidney longed for any sign of him to climb the trellis to her. Why was he being honorable now, when he had not been before? It was his wildness, his namesake, that drew her to him. His spontaneity captured her heart. Sidney closed her eyes, wishing for him. When she opened her eyes, he was not there.

Her fingers flittered through the book, fanning the pages. Her mind was scattered with unspoken emotions she was still coming to grips with. She became distracted from her thoughts when she noticed the scribbles in the columns. The book was new when she lost it, and she had never written in it. When she read the scrawls, they matched Noah's handwriting. She read his notes along the edges, laughing in delight at his comments where he remarked on the hero's foolishness, points he wanted to try with her, and silly words to describe how he interpreted the story.

Sidney slid farther under the covers after she blew out the lantern. She closed the book and held it to her heart, along with his letter. She made the decision to stay in bed. While Wilde gifted her with an apology, she still needed to offer one to him before they met again. Tomorrow she would attempt to right her wrongs with everybody she had hurt tonight. Her eyelids lowered as she thought of a plan. Exhaustion overcame her, and she drifted to sleep with an apology formed in her mind. Tomorrow morning would be soon enough.

~~~~~~

Wilde waited patiently in the garden for her to show him a sign of her forgiveness. When her light disappeared in her bedchamber and she never came to the window, he knew she had not forgiven him. He sat, dejected, on the bench. He hoped for any sign to come his way, but disappointment overwhelmed him when none came. As the night continued, he stayed there, even when the clouds covered the moon and the rain began to fall. He laughed, for it reminded him of the first night he climbed through her window. The rain didn't deter him then, and it wouldn't now. He stood, then snapped off a rose and climbed the trellis.

When he reached her window, he silently slid inside. As he stood, dripping wet, he saw her in a deep sleep. His smile widened when he noticed she gripped his letter and the book in her hands. He hunched down as he watched her sleep. How he wanted to slide under the sheets with her and draw her into his embrace. He wished to whisper to her his deepest desires but knew he couldn't. He didn't want her this way. He wanted her without ruining her. His past actions had done enough of that. Instead, he laid the rose on her opposite pillow. Then he slid a piece of candy from his pocket and tied it around the stem.

With a brush of his fingers across the locks of her hair, he lowered his head to press a gentle kiss to her lips. When she moaned in response and parted her lips, it took everything Wilde had inside him to pull back.

"Noah," she moaned in her sleep.

"Sweet dreams, my Sidney," he whispered in return before he returned to the window.

With one last glance at his love, he climbed back down the trellis and headed to rest on the bench. For the first time in his life, love directed his actions.

Chapter Fifteen

Sophia found her friend sitting at her desk with her research papers spread about, writing rapidly across the parchments. She reclined on the end of the bed unnoticed as Sidney wrote her thesis. Lady Hartridge called on them late this afternoon, begging Sophia to help draw Sidney from her room. From what Lady Hartridge described, Sid had barricaded herself inside her bedchamber since dawn and refused to be disturbed. She locked the door and forbid anybody to enter. Sophia knew of Sid's hiding spot for her key and used it to enter the bedroom.

Sidney worked in a disheveled state, her hair unbound and flowing in wild waves around her face while still dressed in her nightgown. Her robe was inside out. A rose rested on the edge of the desk with a piece of candy tied around the stem. Sophia smiled. Wildeburg drove her friend into a frazzled mess. Finally, a man unbound Sidney's tight restrictions on her frame of mind. Sophia laughed, then her laughter turned louder until her sides ached. Sidney scowled at her interruption but kept on writing. When Sophia realized she couldn't interrupt her friend, she wandered to the windows. As she glanced below, she saw Wildeburg sitting on the bench. When he noticed her, he waved, and Phee waved back.

Sophia swirled around to her friend and noticed a book on the nightstand. Deciding to occupy herself with something to do until Sid finished, she settled on the chaise and opened the book. It was a romance story, the kind Sidney absolutely detested. She sent a puzzled glance her way and then started to read. It was the latest novel in the bookstores. Sophia remembered how Sidney ridiculed the title and the plot of the story. As she flipped through the pages, she noticed small notes written inside. As she brought the book closer to her face, Sidney ripped it from her hands. Sidney swiftly moved the book behind her back to hide it from Sophia's eyes. Sophia, in return, smiled her enjoyment at Sidney's discomfort.

"Romance novels are so cliché. Why do you read such dribble, Phee? They cloud your mind with unreal fantasies," Sophia imitated.

Sidney plopped next to Phee. "I have a confession to make."

"It would appear so," Phee laughed.

"I have secretly devoured romance novels since you read me the first one all those years ago."

"I knew it."

"You did not."

"Well, I wondered anyhow. On some books, you would argue how it wouldn't work for the hero, then not a peep on other novels. You sat entranced as I read to you. Why though?"

"I don't understand why. I guess I wanted to be known for my intellectual mind. If I appeared to read fluff, then those whose respect I hoped to gain would think my mind floated in the clouds."

"Gee, thanks," Phee replied, hurt.

"You misunderstand, Phee. All I possess is my mind while you offer so much more. You're beautiful, kind, and gentlemen hang on your every word. Your grace sets everybody at ease with the right words or gestures. While my charm leans toward offending and arguing with everybody. One look upon your stunning figure and they follow you like a puppy dog. Me, they run the opposite way."

"Nonsense, Sid. You have proven otherwise this season. Since your remarkable change, the gentlemen have flocked to your side. You even had the two most sought after bachelors in the ton pursue you. I think you even managed to catch one of their hearts. The other, well he doesn't deserve any girl. So, what is your opinion of this novel? I have yet to read it."

"I haven't either."

"What about your notes on the side?"

"Those are not mine. Noah stole my book when I saw him in the park."

"When did you meet Lord Wildeburg in the park?"

"The first visit happened after the Woodsworth Ball. Then the next time was the morning after he snuck into my bedroom."

"He snuck into your room more than once?"

"Yes, we've shared a few secret moments together lately."

"How secret?"

"Um, secret enough to ruin me."

"Oh, Sidney."

"Yes, well Sheffield got wind of it, and when Noah didn't come for my hand, Sheffield convinced Papa that a marriage to him would be the best possible solution."

"That underhanded, conceited, manipulative boar," Phee said. She rose and paced the room, mumbling under her breath about the despicable duke.

Sidney lounged on the chaise as Phee built herself into a rage over Sheffield. Something had happened between the two to draw Sophia out of her demure nature. As long as they had been friends, Phee never slandered another soul as much as she had the duke. For Sheffield to draw such emotion from her was almost comical.

"It would appear that I am not the only one holding onto secrets," Sidney said.

Sophia stopped in mid stride, a becoming blush spreading across her cheeks. She could never share with Sid the encounter she had with Sheffield at Madame Bellerose's. It was too intimate in detail. However, that wasn't what kept her from telling Sidney. She couldn't divulge her secret with Sidney when Sheffield didn't realize himself.

"He kissed me in the garden last night."

"He did what? I shouldn't have left you by yourself. Oh, please forgive me, Phee. I sent Rory after you."

"Yes, well, Rory was too late. The duke figured since you offered kisses and he didn't receive his, I should be your substitute."

"Oh, does that man hold no bounds? When I am through with him—"

"No, Sidney, I am fine. I am no worse for wear. Enough about Sheffield. What about Wildeburg?"

"He wrote me a letter of apology. Now I'm writing my thesis, and I am almost finished. I will need your help again. Mama has refused to let me leave the house, and I must go to him."

"Well Sid, you need not go far. He sits below on the bench in your garden. He appears quite wet."

"I'm afraid he has been there since last evening."

"What?"

"Yes, I'm afraid so."

"Oh my. He is in love."

"And so am I."

"Oh, Sid. I am thrilled for both of you."

"Will you assist me one last time?"

Sophia laughed. "Like it will be one last time. We both know I have a lifetime of helping you."

Sidney laughed alongside Phee, realizing she was correct. Still she needed Phee's assistance to sneak from the house and knew her friend would help. She thought of a plan that would require Sophia to persuade Noah to leave her garden. But before all of that, she needed Phee's forgiveness.

"All joking aside, please forgive me for being an awful friend. I recognize something troubles you, and I want to help you first. What is it, Phee?"

In Sophia's excitement for Sidney and Wildeburg, she forgot her own problems. She didn't want to burden Sid with her troubles concerning Sheffield. Sidney would shred Sheffield to pieces. Then Sophia would be ruined, and her father would demand Sheffield to offer for her hand. He was the last gentleman on earth she wanted to be saddled with. No, she would make an excuse to Sidney to appease her.

"It is nothing, Sid. My thoughts on losing you as a friend has saddened me. I saw you falling for Lord Wildeburg and realized it would change the dynamics of our friendship."

"Nonsense, Phee. My love for Noah is because of you, in part. He wrote of your suggestions on how to woo me. Our friendship will never change."

Sidney rose to wrap Phee in a hug. Phee returned her affection, grateful that Sidney believed her false claims. In time, Sophia would figure how to deal with Sheffield. The last thing she needed was for Sid to delve into her problems. Sidney always jumped headfirst into finding a solution. No, she would avoid Sheffield in the future, which should not be too difficult now, considering Sidney's ties with him ended after the fiasco at the Havelock Ball. Phee pulled away from the hug and regarded the stars in Sidney's eyes. She held delight that her friend had found her happily ever after. Now she needed to make sure she lived it.

"What do you need me to do?" Phee asked.

"I need two things from you. First, I need you to deliver my finished thesis to Noah and convince him to return home. Tell him I need one more day before I see him. Explain to him how angry my parents are, and it would be best if he approached a calm house. Make him understand his appearance only fuels my father's anger. He isn't familiar with Papa, so he will believe the small lie. Granted, Papa is angry at him, but Mama and he both find his unwavering attendance romantic."

"And the second thing?"

"Can you help me escape to Noah's house in your carriage? I want to sneak into his bedchamber the same way he has snuck into mine."

"Do you think this is the wisest course of action considering the circumstances of your scandal?"

"Probably not, but I wish to woo him this time around. Only I need your help. Please say yes."

"Yes. Leave Wildeburg and your mama in my hands. First, I will deliver this letter to Wildeburg, then I will distract your mother with some gossip I learned from my mama this morning. It will deliver your mother into such a frenzy that she will forget about you for a few hours. After that, you are on your own."

"You are the best friend in the entire world, Phee."

"Hurry. There isn't much time before darkness falls. I will need to return home soon, or Mama will come looking for me."

~~~~~~

Lord Wildeburg slammed his front door behind him. His butler and a footman rounded the corner at the noise and stopped as they witnessed the scowl on his face. He barked an order at them to retire for the evening, as their services were no longer needed. They swiftly returned to the kitchen, where they informed the rest of the staff of their evening off.

He strode into his study to the liquor cart, where he grabbed the bottle of his finest whiskey and settled into an armchair near the fire. He drank from the bottle, hoping to warm his insides. The fiery liquid set a fire down his throat and into his belly. During the coldest spring on record, he had waited all night and day outside in her garden for a glimpse of her. Nothing. No sign of forgiveness. The only thing he received was a message urging him to return home. Lady Sophia warned him away and handed him a letter of explanation. As he took another swig from the bottle, he pulled the letter from inside his suit pocket. The ink smeared across the front, making the words, *To Noah,* a blurred mess.

He leaned his head against the cushion, closing his eyes in defeat. With a sigh, he broke open the seal to read her letter. Only it wasn't a letter, but an article explaining her thesis.

My theory on the ruination of the young ladies of the ton by Lady Sidney Hartridge:

Whom Shall I Kiss ... An Earl, A Marquess, or a Duke?

I have set out on a personal conquest to expose the scoundrels of the ton and how they ruin young girls after watching many friends fall victim to the rogues who destroyed their reputations. They either had to marry said gentlemen, or their parents sent them away to avoid scandals. I realized it was time to turn the tables on them.

My research was based on three gentlemen from each level of the peerage: An earl, a marquess, and a duke. I chose these three men from the personal exploits I heard from rumor, gossip, or my own personal interactions with them.

The first variable in my research was to change my appearance. If any of you know me, I have never been one to care about my personal appearance, everything from my hair to my style of dress. However, with the help of a close friend, I made a transformation to draw the attentions of my subjects. The result was a success. I drew their interest enough for them to court me in one form or another. I say that because not every courtship was performed in the conventional sense. As you can guess, some were scandalous enough to make even a more experienced lady blush.

As I was saying, I knew one of these gentlemen, for he visited my father frequently. We would become involved in heated debates. He didn't recognize me, even while he danced with me. The second gentleman never met me, but I struck his interest, therefore enticing him to pursue me. The third, while he did recognize me, he began to view me in a different light than he originally had.

While the three gentlemen sought my company, I noticed that if their paths crossed each other, it brought out their competitive sides. They would slander the other while trying to prove they were the better catch. It was not until the end of my research that I discovered the lengths in which they would go to capture my hand.

With two of the gentlemen, they considered me only as a game. A game on which scoundrel could be the first to ruin me. Neither of the men wanted my hand in marriage, but to prove to each other they would be the victor. After they claimed victory, I would mean nothing to them, except for being another lady they ruined. Then they would be off searching for the next contest to compete against.

When I was in each of these gentlemen's company alone, much to my parent's ignorance, I let their charm entice me into exploring my own possible desires. With the first gentleman, I let his rank and attractive appearance draw me into believing in a life we could share. However, his arrogant demeanor soon woke me to what a farce our life would be together. I will admit though, the lure of his kiss beckoned me toward him. There was a moment in the park where he sparked a feeling in ... Well it never happened, and for that I am relieved.

With the third gentleman, his newfound attention flattered my ego. For years, he had been like a member of our family and still is. However, he never once gazed upon me with anything other than friendship or brotherly concern. To realize I could draw the interest from another gorgeous gentleman gave me newfound confidence. I never imagined plain me could have any power over these men. While nothing more transpired than a few touches on the hand and an interest held in his eye, I will be forever in his debt that my experiment hasn't ruined our friendship.

You are probably wondering why I skipped the second gentleman. Well, it is because our time together has become more precious and meaningful to share with anybody else. The moments we spent in each other's company awakened a desire to be loved inside me. Nobody had ever tempted me with the affections he made me feel. I yearn for his kiss and caress even now. I understand we have many obstacles in our way, and we must overcome a scandal most embarrassing for some. But it is not embarrassing for me. Our time spent together never represented a scandal, but if it is, I wish to cause many more.

In conclusion, my research has become clouded with an uninformed bias toward my subjects. I am unable to reach a conclusion based on my heart's discovery of love. With that, I have proven my thesis false by my own sabotage of the facts. I hope nobody can prove my theory. I wish for all the gentlemen and the ladies of the ton to explore their passions and find a love like I did.

Wilde laughed in joy at her paper. He had hope. She declared her love for him. Sidney Hartridge loved him. He needed to see her now. Wilde rose and strode from his study, calling for his servants to ready a bath for him. When his house echoed with no response, he remembered giving them the night off. Well that wouldn't stop him. He took the stairs two at a time as he ran to his chambers.

He flung open the door and his footsteps faltered at a crunch beneath his feet. He knelt and picked up a piece of candy. Butterscotch. In fact, a trail of sweets led a path to his bed. When his glance rose, he noticed his open windows exposed the last of the fading sun. His heartbeat jumped when he saw the reason for the open window and the trail of candy. There, under the blanket, lay the object of his love. He paused, hoping it wasn't a figment of his imagination when she dropped the sheet and beckoned him with the crook of her finger. Wilde followed her command and gathered the sweet confections along the way. He set them on the bedside table with an idea for later. For now, he wanted to confess his love to her.

"Sidney—"

"Shh," she replied, tugging him toward her.

She wrapped her arms around him as she brought her lips to his for a kiss. Her fingers went to work divesting him of his clothing. She lay naked under his touch and wanted to touch him too. Her need for him became more powerful than words. They didn't need to speak. There would be time to talk later. When he didn't object and his kiss became hungrier, Sidney's heart slowed. As she waited for him, she allowed her fear to worry her with thoughts. What if she misjudged his intentions? But when she sensed his need as strong as her own, it calmed her enough to coax him into long, sensuous kisses that drew out their passion.

Wilde calmed as her kisses slowed. He savored the sweet flavor of butterscotch on her lips as her kisses drugged him. He drew her along his body as his mouth devoured her, tasting her love. Each slow brush of his tongue matched hers, each nip of her lips promised more. Each touch of her hand sent him to a higher need to be one with her. When she slid her hand down to his hardness, he groaned deeply into her mouth. Her innocent touch explored him as he fought his desire to take her. He pulled away from her mouth and kissed his way along her neck to her breasts as she stroked him higher. He drew her nipple between his lips and sucked gently, building her desire and need. When she moaned and her strokes became faster, he slid his hand between her thighs.

Slowly his fingers slid inside her, drawing out her moans as his touch pleasured her. Each pull of his finger inside her was slow and made her ache for more. When his tongue licked her nipples, she desired more. After he slid in another finger and stroked her, she raised her body to him, begging him for more. She tightened her grip on him as his stroke sent the flame inside her to another level. As her need intensified, he sucked her nipples harder. That was when Sidney realized how her desire affected him. They were both consumed with a passion that built with each stroke of a finger or a kiss. She desired more from him which only he could give her.

"Last time you mentioned something with your tongue, and you also referenced it in my novel with your side notes," she tempted him.

Wilde raised his head to stare in her eyes, her boldness beckoning him. He guided his fingers deep inside her, her wetness coating them as he moved them. He watched her midnight blue eyes darken with need. "Here?" he questioned her as he slid his fingers into his mouth, licking off her sweet taste.

Her eyes widened, never had she read anything as scandalous as his actions. When his tongue caressed her wetness from his fingers, her core ached for more. She moaned as he returned his fingers to fulfill her need. She arched her hips, guiding his touch in deeper when he groaned. He spread her thighs wide as he settled in between them. After he lowered his head, his mouth consumed her. He hungrily licked her wetness, drawing her ache to a new level. His licks grew stronger and bolder, each stroke of his tongue faster as her wetness flowed. Noah built her ache high, and then paused. His tongue slowly slid along her core, lightly flicking. When his tongue settled on her clit, he stroked the tight bud in small circles. Sidney begged him for more.

Wilde heard her pleading moans, but he couldn't get enough of her. He couldn't quench his thirst. He grabbed her hips and brought her core to his mouth as he glided his tongue inside her, slowly stroking in and out, drawing her wetness into his mouth. Yet, he needed more. When she tried to pump against his mouth, he held her still. He sensed her need on edge as he drove her to new heights. He wanted to drink from her as she flew over the edge. As he stroked his tongue in and out, his thumb found her clit and caressed the tight bud back and forth as she exploded underneath him. He drank from the desire she gifted him.

As her body floated in the mass of clouds, he continued his onslaught to her affections. Each kiss to her skin as he moved up her body built her desire again. As he settled over her, he drew her lips in a kiss. The essence of her on his lips mingled with the butterscotch from her. When he slid deep inside, she moaned in his kiss. As his body stroked her into an ache again, she clasped him closer.

Wilde felt the need consume her again as her wetness clung around him. He drew each stroke nice and long as she clung to him tighter. His mouth ravished her lips, building on their desire as he felt her throb around his cock. He wrapped her legs around his waist when his strokes became faster and harder. His need for her consumed him. The taste of her in his mouth still lingered. His ache grew more as her hips matched him with each stroke.

"Noah," she moaned, "please."

Her plea undid him, he could no longer hold back. He slid in hard and held himself, rotating in small circles as she gasped her pleasure. Then he held still and stared into her eyes.

"I love you, Sidney."

She slid her palm over his cheek. "I love you too, Noah," she whispered, kissing him gently.

He closed his eyes at her gentle touch and words. The emotions of forgiveness and love floated around them. Their bodies moved as one as they met each other with each slow stroke of their bodies. When they reached the heights they climbed together, they floated together in their bliss.

As they held each other, Noah slid his fingers through her hair and asked her the same question as last time. "Why?"

"I wanted to experience how it felt to climb through a window and seduce a scoundrel. Research for my next project."

He rolled her over and scowled at her. "I will be your only subject for that research."

"On all research, I would imagine." Sidney gave Noah a kiss to soothe him.

"When will you publish your paper?" he asked as he settled with her in his arms.

She rolled over and placed her hands on his chest. "Never. I could never hurt those involved, with the exception of Sheffield."

"Are you sure? I will stand by your side if you wish to do so."

"I know you would. No, the paper is only for my records."

"You shouldn't be so hard on Sheffield. You were too tempting to resist."

"I can almost forgive him for his role he played with you, since I did the same. But I cannot forgive him for the hurt he inflicted on my friend. Something played out between him and Sophia, and I aim to discover what."

"Perhaps it would be wise to let them handle it themselves."

"No, she is my friend and needs my help."

"Is this going to be our life?"

"What life?"

"Our life together."

"What, sneaking into each other's windows?"

"There will be no sneaking when we share the same window."

"Funny, I do not recall your offer."

Wilde brought her hands to his lips and kissed her ring finger. "Will you do me the honor of becoming my bride, Sidney Hartridge?"

"You realize once we are married you will need to think of your own material. Not the ones you read from my romance novels or from the help of my best friend."

"Funny, I didn't hear you complaining earlier on my own material. In fact, I seem to recall you begging for more."

Sidney swatted at him as she blushed at the memory. The memory lingered in her mind, growing into a desire for him to educate her on more of his material. When her eyes changed, he growled his agreement, pulling her to him for a kiss. She asked if he had more to share, and he whispered that he possessed a lifetime of knowledge to share with her. His kisses held the promise of more as he swept her away on another flood of desire.

Epilogue

"Are you sure about this, Sidney?"

"Trust me, I am never wrong with my instincts."

"I feel we shouldn't interfere."

"Nonsense, something simmers between them, and I mean to uncover their connection."

Wilde drew Sidney into his arms. "Shouldn't we worry about our own connection, Lady Wildeburg?"

"Why, Lord Wildeburg, again so soon?"

Noah nibbled on Sidney's neck as he tried to distract her from her latest project, but he couldn't deter her. As much of an enticement he was, she needed to secure her friend's happiness.

Noah pulled back after he finished kissing his wife. "If this dinner is not a success and I prove you wrong, will you promise to halt your plans for Sophia?"

"I promise, but I know I am not."

"Very well. Until this evening, My Lady."

"I will make it up to you later, My Lord, and that is a promise I will keep." Sidney kissed him before she floated out of his study.

"Promise? Keep? Sidney," Noah growled.

Sidney popped her head around the door. "Yes, dear?"

Noah shook his head at her innocent expression. Since they married, he became aware of her interfering nature. While done in goodness, she seemed to cause more trouble than anything else. Her curious mind on human behavior would keep him entertained for years to come.

"Nothing, darling."

"One more thing, dear."

"Yes?"

"Please keep Sheffield away from Sophia this evening. I don't need him to ruin my plans. I only invited him for you and to show there were no hard feelings. If he so much as oversteps his welcome, I will not hesitate to rewrite my thesis and publish it in all the newspapers."

"I will keep Sheffield occupied."

"That is why I love you so."

"The only reason?"

"Well, no ..." Sidney replied as she stepped back into his study, locking the door behind her.

Sidney spent the rest of the afternoon showing her other reasons for loving Noah Wildeburg with all her heart. Wilde, in return, showed her a few new reasons of his own. Sidney forgot about her arrangements as they expressed their love for one another.

Read Sophia's story in *Whom Shall I Marry... An Earl or A Duke?*

"Thank you for reading Whom Shall I Kiss... An Earl, A Marquess, or A Duke? Gaining exposure as an independent author relies mostly on

word-of-mouth, so if you have the time and inclination, please consider leaving a short review wherever you can."

Visit my website www.lauraabarnes.com to join my mailing list

Author Laura A. Barnes

International selling author Laura A. Barnes fell in love with writing in the second grade. After her first creative writing assignment, she knew what she wanted to become. Many years went by with Laura filling her head full of story ideas and some funny fish songs she wrote while fishing with her family. Thirty-seven years later, she made her dreams a reality. With her debut novel *Rescued By the Captain*, she has set out on the path she always dreamed about.

When not writing, Laura can be found devouring her favorite romance books. Laura is married to her own Prince Charming (who for some reason or another thinks the heroes in her books are about him) and they have three wonderful children and two sweet grandbabies. Besides her love of reading and writing, Laura loves to travel. With her passport stamped in England, Scotland, and Ireland; she hopes to add more countries to her list soon.

While Laura isn't very good on the social media front, she loves to hear from her readers. You can find her on the following platforms:

You can visit her at *www.lauraabarnes.com* to join her mailing list.

Website: **http://www.lauraabarnes.com**
Amazon: **https://amazon.com/author/lauraabarnes**
Goodreads: **https://www.goodreads.com/author/show/16332844.Laura_A_Barnes**
Facebook: **https://www.facebook.com/AuthorLauraA.Barnes/**
Instagram: **https://www.instagram.com/labarnesauthor/**
Twitter: **https://twitter.com/labarnesauthor**
BookBub: **https://www.bookbub.com/profile/laura-a-barnes**

Desire other books to read by Laura A. Barnes

Enjoy these other historical romances:

Matchmaking Madness Series:

How the Lady Charmed the Marquess

Tricking the Scoundrels Series:

Whom Shall I Kiss... An Earl, A Marquess, or A Duke?

Whom Shall I Marry... An Earl or A Duke?

I Shall Love the Earl

The Scoundrel's Wager

The Forgiven Scoundrel

Romancing the Spies Series:

Rescued By the Captain

Rescued By the Spy

Rescued By the Scot

.